The Princess Rules

IT'S A PRINCE THING

First published in Great Britain by
HarperCollins *Children's Books* in 2020
HarperCollins *Children's Books* is a division of HarperCollins*Publishers* Ltd,
HarperCollins Publishers
1 London Bridge Street
London SE1 9GF

The HarperCollins website address is
www.harpercollins.co.uk

1

ISBN 978–0–00–840325–6

Philippa Gregory and Chris Chatterton assert the moral right to be identified
as the author and illustrator of the work respectively.
A CIP catalogue record for this title is available from the British Library.

Printed and bound in England by CPI Group (UK) Ltd, Croydon CR0 4YY

MIX
Paper from
responsible sources
FSC
www.fsc.org **FSC™ C007454**

This book is produced from independently certified FSC™ paper
to ensure responsible forest management.

For more information visit: www.harpercollins.co.uk/green

The Princess Rules

IT'S A PRINCE THING

PHILIPPA GREGORY

Illustrations by

Chris Chatterton

HarperCollins *Children's Books*

For Freddie and Sebastian

Contents

Florizella and the Brother

CHAPTER ONE

*Even fairytale land has
trouble with deliveries*

There was a tiny silver moon, as thin as a rind, when the queen of the Seven Kingdoms heard a tap on the bedroom window. She opened it, and found a tired and very bored stork balancing on the windowsill with a big parcel under one wing.

'Sign here,' his beak yawned as he pushed a scroll with wax seals at her.

'I don't think that we . . .' said the queen.

'King? Did you order anything?'

But the king was singing in the bath and did not hear her.

The stork shoved a fat parcel into her hands.

'Oh! But this is for the king and queen of the Far Away Mountains!' the queen protested, reading the label. 'It's not for us.'

'They're not at home,' said the stork. 'You're their registered safe place.'

'Yes, but . . .'

The stork flew off into the night. It was his last delivery. 'I shouldn't be working this late,' she could hear him complaining as he disappeared into the darkness. 'Anybody would think I was an owl!'

'Bother the king and queen of the Far Away Mountains!' said the queen. 'They're always

getting their stuff left here. I don't know why they can't leave it under the drawbridge like everybody else . . .' Then she ripped the fastening of the parcel and said, 'OH!' And then she said, 'It's a baby.'

It was the most adorable little prince that anyone had ever seen. The queen, who already had one child – a daughter called Florizella – was delighted to have another. 'Look what's arrived!' she said as the king came out of the bathroom. 'We've got a baby prince at last.'

'Good thing too!' said the king. 'Excellent! Excellent!' And he got into bed and went to sleep at once, while the queen dressed the baby in the royal christening gown and put him in the royal cradle and rocked him gently.

 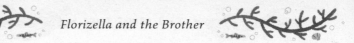

In the morning the baby had grown and was about the size of a four-year-old child. 'It seems like only yesterday that he was a baby,' the queen said.

'It was yesterday, wasn't it?' the king asked. 'You'd better hurry up and get him christened if he's going to grow this quickly.'

So the queen invited everyone in the kingdom and sent the messages out by a flock of pelicans. She was just posting the last envelope into the huge open beak of the last pelican when Princess Florizella came into the room.

'What's this?' Florizella asked, looking from the windowsill where the flock of pelicans were squatting, beaks bulging with invitations, to the little boy sitting on the floor and building a train set.

'This is the new king of the Seven Kingdoms!' The king was delighted.

'Your little brother!' the queen exclaimed.

'Prince . . .' The king paused – he could not think of a name. 'What shall we call him, my dear?' he asked. 'Usually you call a prince after the circumstances of his birth. So I was christened Prince Gooseberry – because my parents found me under a gooseberry bush. And Florizella's friend was called Prince Bonnet because his mother found him in a hatbox.'

'Bennett,' Florizella said. 'His name's Bennett.'

'He didn't like Bonnet for some reason,' her mother explained. 'So, what shall we call this boy – who came to us by mistake of the delivery stork?'

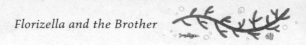

'Prince Courier,' the king said happily. 'Good name. And then King Courier – has quite a ring to it.'

'Hang on a minute,' Florizella said. 'What d'you mean "king"?'

'Well, of course, he'll be king when we're gone,' the king said cheerfully. 'Won't you?' He picked up the little boy and bounced him up and down on his knee. 'Um-tiddly-um! Who's a little king then?'

'Hang on a minute,' said Florizella again. 'It's me who inherits the kingdom. This is my kingdom, and my palace, and everything.'

'Yes, but now we've got a boy, a prince,' the queen said. 'Boys come before girls. Everyone knows that.' She saw that Florizella was looking astonished. 'You know that, Florizella.'

'I know it IN THEORY,' Florizella said carefully. She looked at Prince Courier. 'IN THEORY is when it is a plan, or a thought, or even a fairy story. But it's a very different thing when you see it happening in real life. It's especially different when you see it happening in your own life.'

'Where are you going?' the queen asked as Florizella headed for the door.

'I'm going to see another prince,' Florizella said crossly. 'On my pony. Unless, of course, he's Courier's pony now?'

CHAPTER TWO

*In which Florizella learns
of the risk she took by
being born a girl*

*P*rince Bennett was in a hammock in the orchard of his palace, reading a fairy tale, when Florizella marched in. 'Hi, Florizella!' he said as soon as he saw her. 'You know, the weirdest things happen in books . . .'

'Something rather weird has happened here as well,' Florizella said shortly.

'Great!' Bennett said. 'I love it when

something happens. Was it SUDDENLY? I like it best when it's SUDDENLY. Are we going on an adventure? Shall I get my sword?'

'It's more of a thinking adventure,' Florizella said. 'Bennett – if you had an older sister, would she be queen and you stay prince all your life?'

'No,' Bennett said. 'I'd be the king and she'd stay a princess all her life unless she was lucky enough to marry a king. That's the Prince Permit. You know: princesses have the Princess Rules and we princes have the Prince Permit, which tells us how everything happens and everything we should do.'

Florizella was fascinated. 'I knew about the Princess Rules, because I had to learn them and everyone wanted me to obey them, but

not about the Prince Permit. What sort of things do princes have to do?'

Bennett laughed. 'We don't have to do anything! It's a permit – it allows us to do things; it's not like rules that tell you what you can't do. It's a prince thing. We get the throne, no matter how many older sisters we have, and we write the laws – no matter what people say about them. We own all the land and we get really, really rich, but we never, ever talk about it. We get a twenty-one gun salute on our birthday, and people bow to us. We're first in the charge into battle but last into lifeboats – I think the lifeboats is the only time we're ever at the back of the queue, and of course that hardly ever happens. We get to fight all the dragons and monsters, while princesses can only watch. We get the best horse and we get to choose our bride. She can't choose us, and she can't say "no". We can behead people if we want to. You know, just regular prince stuff.'

'But that's not fair,' Florizella said. 'I get the Princess Rules, and you get a whole load of permissions?'

Prince Bennett shrugged. 'It's not fair at all!' he agreed happily. 'It's completely in favour of princes. But it's always been like that, so nobody questions it—'

'I'm questioning it!' Florizella interrupted him.

'Yes. But we princes don't. And most people don't even think about it because it's always been this way. Best of all is when they say it's "natural". As if us getting first place in everything is how it's always been, and always has to be.'

'But it *isn't* natural!' Florizella exclaimed. 'It's been made up so princesses don't get a fair chance at things! It was invented by princes, and enforced by kings!'

'I know!' Bennett grinned. 'And we can be bad princes too – which princesses never are. We can be bad kings. We can grind the poor—'

'Grind them?'

'Be mean to them. We can declare wars for no reason, we can be tyrants and tell everyone what to do, and if people object, we can say that's treason, and cut their heads off. It's just great being a prince.'

'I can't be a bad princess,' Florizella said regretfully. 'A princess can get locked up in an unscalable tower for just being eighteen. Imagine what people would do to a princess who was actually bad!'

'Put her to sleep in a glass coffin?' Bennett suggested.

'Snow White got that just for being pretty,' Florizella said gloomily. 'Little Red Riding Hood got swallowed by a wolf just for visiting her granny.'

'And Sleeping Beauty . . .' Bennett reminded her.

'Don't even get me started on Sleeping Beauty! But anyway – that's not what's just happened.'

'Something's happened? Oh! Yes! You said. Was it SUDDENLY?'

'It *was* rather suddenly,' Florizella agreed. 'We've suddenly got a prince. A mistaken delivery. It was supposed to go somewhere else.'

'Take it round to them?' Bennett suggested. 'When they're in?'

'I thought of that, but they don't want it. They meant to order a Baby Belling, not a real baby. It was a substitution. A really bad substitution.'

'What's a Baby Belling?'

'A sort of cooker,' Florizella said gloomily. 'So you can see they don't want a real baby. But my parents really do. And they're saying he's going to be king. Of MY kingdom.'

'Well – that's the risk you take,' Bennett said cheerfully. 'When you're born a girl.'

'But I don't want to take that risk,' Florizella replied. 'I didn't mean to take it.'

'Those are the Princess Rules,' Bennett replied. 'Like the Prince Permit – it's just how it's always been done in fairytale land.'

'Well, I don't obey the Princess Rules,' Florizella objected. 'You know I don't. I have my own horse, Jellybean; I've killed my own dragon. I get a twenty-one gun salute on my birthday, all to myself. And I am going to inherit the Land of the Seven Kingdoms.'

'You *were* going to inherit the Land of the Seven Kingdoms,' Bennett corrected. 'But not any more! Not now they've got a prince.'

Florizella thought hard. 'Well, this is one

Princess Rule I'm going to break for sure,' she said. 'I'm not giving up my kingdom.'

'Then you'll have to teach your little brother not to use his Prince Permit,' Bennett said. 'Because the Prince Permit says that boys are better than girls, that they become king whether or not there is a girl. And you're going to hate that.'

'We'll both teach him,' Florizella decided.

'Whoa! Not me!' Bennett took a step back.

'Yes, you,' Florizella said firmly. 'If you're a real prince, a true prince, then you'll want things to be fair. A real prince cares about sharing and everyone being happy, doesn't he?'

Bennett thought for a moment. He did care about Florizella and he did want to make things fair. He did think that girls were as good as boys and should have an equal chance. 'I s'pose so,' he said thoughtfully. 'But we're going against all the fairy tales ever told . . .'

'We are,' Florizella agreed. 'Let's do it!'

CHAPTER THREE

*Unfortunately, Courier
thinks that Prince
Permits are great*

*F*irst things first: in order to teach Prince
Courier, they had to get hold of him.

'We can't just take him out of his cradle!'
Florizella said. 'I know that's not allowed.'

But actually, when she went to look, the
prince had grown again, and wasn't there. He
no longer fitted the royal cradle.

'How they shoot up,' the king said fondly.
'Look, Florizella, he's going to be taller than you.'

'Yes,' Florizella agreed. 'By tomorrow at this rate. But that still wouldn't make him king. Because if it was just about how tall you were, then basketball players would be kings. If it was about how strong you were, then all the kings would be weight lifters – and that isn't so.'

'Undoubtedly!' said the king who was quite short and rounded. *'Undootedly!'*

'So, you agree that it doesn't matter how big you are to be king?' said Florizella.

'No,' the king agreed. 'It doesn't matter how big you are.'

'And it doesn't matter how strong you are to be king?'

'No,' he said cautiously.

'Then why should it matter if you're a girl or a boy, or anything else?'

The king stroked his chin and looked thoughtful. 'It's a tradition, that's why,' he said. 'Dating back to the time when kings did everything and princesses were mostly goose girls, or sometimes servants. Or sometimes they were hardly people at all but grew out of fish or flowers. Some of them were locked up in towers that they couldn't climb down. Quite a few were fast asleep until they were woken up by the prince. Poor things! Fancy having your birthday and falling asleep in the middle of your first ever party, and not waking up for a hundred years! Girls are so ridiculous!' The king laughed and when he saw Florizella's face he turned it into a cough. 'Poor things,' he said more seriously. 'Terrible, really.'

'Those days are gone,' Florizella said firmly.

'Long gone. Can we take Courier out for a walk?'

'You can take him for a ride on his pony,' the king said.

'He's got a pony? Why has he got a pony all of a sudden?'

'He's a prince!' said the king. 'He gets everything.'

So they all went out on their ponies to the Purple Forest and showed Courier where Florizella had found the wolf cub, Samson, who now lived at the palace, and where a dragon had found Prince Bennett. As they rode home Bennett said very nicely, 'Look here, Courier, you can't be king you know; it's Florizella's kingdom.'

'I did wonder,' Courier said cautiously. 'But it seemed as though all I had to do was just turn up and get everything.'

'Well, you can't.' Florizella had been feeling a bit awkward about saying that the kingdom was hers – which is odd really, since it *was* hers, and always had been. But it is sometimes hard to stand up for yourself, even if you are a princess. She had not yet learned that one of the lessons of being a princess is learning to stand up for yourself. You can do it quite nicely.

'But it's called a kingdom,' Courier pointed out. 'So it sounds as though it should naturally be for a king. For *me*!'

'The name will have to change too,' Florizella said.

'And there are a few other things about the Prince Permit that we might as well get rid of,' Bennett suggested. 'While we're at it.'

'Like what?' Courier asked. 'Don't be too hasty,

Bennett. It seems pretty good to me. I've been studying it. Princes go first into battle, we get the best horse—'

'But, Courier, that's the point. It's not fair that princes get everything just because they're boys,' Bennett interrupted.

'And vice versa,' Florizella offered. 'We'll rewrite the Princess Rules too. I want it to be fair for boys and girls.'

'Why? Do girls get anything that boys don't have?' Courier asked, interested.

Florizella thought for a moment. 'Dancing lessons?'

Bennett shook his head. 'I can tell you: boys get dancing lessons. I had to dance with one hundred and twenty princesses at my princess-choosing ball. I had lessons. For months.'

'We get girls' toys,' Florizella said. 'Dolls to dress up and cuddle.'

'Isn't that just to teach you how to be a mum?' Courier asked. 'So that you have something to do while I'm being king?'

'We get to wear dresses?'

'I would really like a great dress,' Courier agreed. 'A long one that goes swish.'

'We can wear dresses if we want,' Bennett pointed out. 'We just call them robes. I have some fantastic capes. And wow! You should see my uniforms. I'm an admiral.'

'What's that?' Courier asked. 'Could I be one?'

'Course you could,' Bennett said. 'The Prince Permit says so. You can be an admiral and a general.'

'People give us play kitchens? And pretend food,' Florizella continued. 'And nurse uniforms.'

'That's mum-training again,' Courier told her.

It was surprising, Florizella thought, how much Courier knew about everything, given that he'd only recently been delivered to the wrong address by an overtired stork. 'How come you're such an expert?' she asked.

Courier shrugged. 'The Prince Permit,' he said. 'Boys act like they know everything.'

'And anyway,' said Bennett. 'Boys can play kitchens. We can be chefs, really important shouty chefs.'

'We have long hair that we can braid and plait?' It was Florizella's last point and her heart wasn't really in it.

The boys just shrugged. They did not want plaits and if they had wanted them, they could have grown their hair as long as any girl anyway.

'I have beautiful curls,' Courier said nonchalantly. 'The queen says I have golden curls like a princess.'

'I know you do,' Florizella said through her teeth. 'I think everyone knows. I think they have been pointed out to everyone who came to your christening. Several times.'

'Well, I wouldn't know, because I've only just arrived, but I don't think girls get anything especially good, do they?' Courier asked. 'Boys get loads of things: swords and army toys, tools and train sets, footballs and boxing gloves, and uniforms. When we grow up we can be firefighters and pilots, astronauts and engine drivers, wrestlers and kings.'

'Girls can have all of those things, and be all of those things too!' Florizella insisted.

'Yes, but it's not expected of them,' Bennett pointed out. 'People don't talk to girls about doing it, and tell them they should do it, and tell them their mothers did it, and it runs in the family. And then, when girls do something good but normal, everyone makes a huge fuss about it and says they're the only girl ever to do it and how come they did? And did their dad teach them? But being brilliant and owning loads of stuff and being fantastically brave and clever is what you aim for if you're a regular boy. It seems like girls have to be ten times better at everything to get the same rewards as a boy.'

'And then, if anything goes wrong, everyone says that it doesn't come naturally to you,' Florizella said gloomily.

'You know, I wasn't born yesterday . . .' Courier started.

'Day before,' Florizella reminded him.

'But that can't be right,' said Courier.

CHAPTER FOUR

Suddenly,
something happens

They rode in silence for a little while, thinking about everything they'd talked about, when suddenly there was a crash and a clatter, like someone riding very fast through the bushes towards them.

'Watch out!' Florizella exclaimed. 'Something's coming, and it's coming very fast!'

'Suddenly!' Bennett said, pleased. 'My favourite word! Stand fast!'

Florizella and Bennett got either side of Prince Courier on his smaller pony, and they turned to face the danger.

'We've got no swords,' Bennett said crossly. 'I thought we were just going out for a ride.'

'I've got a dagger in my boot,' Florizella said.

'Course you have,' Bennett said enviously as five horse riders rode out of the forest, scaring the birds and frightening Courier's pony. 'D'you always carry it?'

'Course I do,' Florizella replied.

'Stand and deliver!' Courier shouted at the horse riders.

'What does he mean?' Bennett asked Florizella over her little brother's head. 'Does he think he's a highwayman?'

'No idea,' she said. 'He's very keen on

deliveries – because of how we got him. I think he means "Halt!".'

'I DO! That's what I mean!' Courier shouted. 'Halt! Who goes there?'

'We're a kidnapping party,' the riders said helpfully. 'Sir.'

'What?' Bennett yelped.

'We've come to kidnap the new prince,' the first man said. 'We heard that the Land of the Seven Kingdoms had a prince at last. So we're going to kidnap him. If you could just hand him over, then we'll take him off to our villainous lair, and wait for the sacks of gold for ransom money.'

'You never kidnapped me,' Florizella pointed out.

The man shrugged. 'Hardly worth the

effort,' he said. 'A princess ransom? Not worth saddling up the horses. Now – is that him? Hand him over!'

'Never! He goes nowhere without us!' Florizella threatened. She meant the man to understand that he would have to fight them for Prince Courier but, instead, it seemed he was perfectly agreeable to the idea of kidnapping them all.

'Just as you like,' he said. 'Since you're all here.'

And the man behind him giggled. 'Three for the price of one!'

'Who are you?' a kidnapping woman asked. 'Before we go to all the trouble of seizing you?'

'Princess Florizella and Prince Bennett,' Courier told them.

'Oh! The old princess.' She was very unimpressed.

Florizella looked at Bennett. 'Are there rules for old princesses too?'

He nodded. 'It's even worse for old ones. They have to live with no one but cats in a wood.'

While the first man kept an arrow pointed at Courier's head, the others took the ponies' reins and tied Florizella up in knots, before lashing Prince Courier to his saddle. As they turned towards Bennett the prince made his horse rear up on its hind legs; it was just brilliant. The kidnappers jumped back in fright, just for a moment, and Bennett whirled his horse round and dashed away.

'He's running away?' Courier looked at Florizella.

'Running away isn't very princely! Shouldn't he have fought everyone and freed us?'

'Thinking not fighting,' Florizella advised him. 'He'll have gone to get help.'

Courier turned to the kidnappers. 'I'm hungry,' he said.

Florizella was surprised. The Princess Rules were very clear that 'Princesses Live Off Air' and 'Princes Feast Like Kings'. So she understood that Courier had a right to get anything he wanted. But she didn't expect him to be whining for biscuits in the middle of a kidnap attempt.

'I want sweeties,' he said. 'Sweeties!'

Florizella was beginning to find Prince Courier most unheroic. 'Get a grip, Courier,' she hissed.

'I won't go anywhere without sweeties!' he said, and he opened his mouth to make a great loud bellow.

'No crying,' Florizella reminded him. 'It's in the Prince Permit – no cry babies.'

'I don't see why not,' he said, as one of the kidnappers produced a huge bag of sweeties and thrust them into Courier's hands. 'See? It gets you what you want. Anyway, I think I should be allowed to express my feelings.'

'No cry babies,' repeated Florizella, who was feeling that there was something to be said for the old Prince Permit, if it kept small brothers quiet.

'You've got to loosen the rope,' Courier whined to the kidnappers. 'What's the good of me having a bag of sweets, if I can't eat them?'

Sighing, because it had been no more
than ten minutes but they were already fed
up of looking after children, the
kidnappers loosened the rope, got
on their horses, and led the way
deep into the Purple Forest.
Florizella followed them, her
hands and feet tied to her saddle
on her most dejected pony
Jellybean. Courier's pony
was jogging behind, with
Courier eating sweets so
clumsily that he was
dropping as many
as he ate.

CHAPTER FIVE

Surprisingly, it is Courier who delivers a brilliant victory

The kidnappers had a hideaway camp near the top of a mountain, deep in the forest, well hidden from any rescue party. As they reached it a kidnapper said to Florizella, 'Ha-ha-ha! Nobody will ever find you here.'

'And,' said another, tying her to a tree, 'you will never escape.'

Florizella, who had not forgotten the dagger in her boot, said nothing. But Prince Courier, who was tied beside her, started to whimper.

'Oh, do be quiet,' Florizella said crossly. It wasn't very nice of her but she was learning to be a big sister, and she had only had a brother for three days. 'Crying won't help.'

'But I'm cold!' Prince Courier cried in a whiny voice. 'Why don't you light a fire?'

'In case there is a rescue party and they see the smoke,' one of the kidnappers said.

'Just a little fire, and there'll be hardly any smoke,' Courier pleaded. 'Or I'll cry and cry and then I'll probably be sick.'

'Oh, all right, if you're such a softie,' the kidnapper said.

Florizella thought of telling Courier to man up; but she truly believed bravery was something that anyone could do. Same as being a bit weedy – boys and girls could be either, or a bit of both, whatever they thought best. Besides, now that the kidnappers had found some dry wood and lit a fire, it was rather cosy, and Courier had stopped complaining and fallen asleep.

The kidnappers found it cosy too, for first they warmed themselves, then they wrapped themselves up in blankets and lay down before the fire, and within moments everyone was fast asleep.

All except Florizella.

And, as it turned out, all except Florizella and her little brother. For Courier had been pretending to be asleep. In fact, he had been wide awake all along. 'Have you still got your dagger?' he whispered in a very different voice from the whiny spoiled-prince voice he had been using.

'Yes, of course,' Florizella said, surprised. 'Are you all right now? Don't want sweeties or a fire lit?'

'Course I am! I was always all right. Can you get the dagger out of your boot and cut the knots at my wrists?'

Prince Courier wriggled backwards to his sister and held out his bound arms. She bent over her feet and got the dagger from her boot with her teeth. Then holding the hilt between her feet, and with Courier leaning backwards over the blade, they managed to saw through the ties that bound his hands. Then it was quick work, once his hands were free, for him to take the dagger and cut

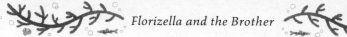 

through the ropes that tied his feet together.

'Me now!' Florizella hissed at him. 'Women and children first!'

He shook his head. 'I'll gallop off and get help like Bennett. You stay here, tied up, like a princess.'

'You know that makes no sense at all,' she hissed at him. 'You cut my ropes too.'

Quickly and quietly he freed Florizella.

'Now,' he said. 'Help me heave our blankets on to the fire.'

'Wha—?'

'For smoke,' he said, and so they took all the blankets they had been given and threw them on to the flames. They took the blankets from the horses too, and burned them as well. At once the fire belched out great clouds of white smoke up into the sky, a clear signal to anyone who might be looking. Florizella grabbed Courier's arm and the two of them dived into the undergrowth.

'What now?' Courier asked her.

'Up a tree, I think,' Florizella said. 'I don't know our way home, and I'm sure Bennett will be coming to the rescue. He'll see the smoke signal and come in this direction.'

'Oh, he'll find us all right,' Courier said certainly. 'I set a trail.'

'You did?'

'I dropped peppermints all the way here.'

Florizella looked at her little brother with something like respect. 'You did? But why peppermints? Because they are white and shiny and showed up in the mud?'

'Nope.' He shook his head – he was still a little prince, not a big one yet. 'I don't like peppermints,' he said. 'I didn't mind dropping them. I wasn't going to drop the jellies, was I?'

Florizella shook her head in disbelief. 'Up you go,' she said, pushing him up into a tall pine tree.

Up, up he went, and Florizella followed after him. They settled themselves into the crook of a branch many metres up, and watched the smoke streaming into the sky while the kidnappers slept below – none of them knowing that their hiding place had been betrayed by the Prince Courier bonfire and the Prince Courier peppermint trail.

*P*rince Bennett galloped into the palace of the Seven Kingdoms over the drawbridge, yelling at the top of his voice. 'Princess Florizella has been captured. Prince Courier too!'

The captain of the guard caught the reins of his pony. 'What?' she snapped.

'Princess Florizella –' pant, pant – 'kidnappers . . . Prince Courier too –' pant – 'in the Purple Forest . . . deep in the forest . . . Captain Stella,' Bennett gasped.

'But where?' she asked. It was a huge forest and most of it had no paths at all, and any paths almost always led to swamps and deep quarries. 'Where exactly?'

Bennett looked back in despair at the road that he had thundered down, and at the great haze of the huge forest. Of course, they could be anywhere; it would be almost impossible to find them. Bennett and the captain looked again towards the endless horizon of the forest. And, as if in answer to their question, a tall tower of smoke slowly bloomed and then hung in the air above the forest. It was as though an arrow was pointing down towards the kidnappers' bonfire.

'There, I should think,' Bennett said, pointing.

'I should think so too,' said the captain of the

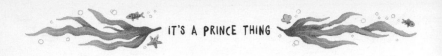

guard. 'Sound the alarm! Turn out the guard!
Mount and ride!'

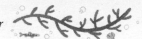

Bennett very much admired the captain of the guard. 'Can I come too?' he asked politely. 'Please may I? Captain Stella?'

'I'm counting on you,' she said, and swung up on to her big horse. She pushed back her cape so it rippled behind her as she led the guard at a canter, over the drawbridge and down the road to the Purple Forest. She called over her shoulder to Bennett. 'Your Highness! Lead the way into the forest; take us on the path that you rode down.'

'Aye aye, Captain,' Bennett said, getting his reply confused in his excitement. 'I mean – Yes! Ma'am!'

Quickly, Bennett retraced the path that he,

Florizella and Courier had ridden earlier. That was easy; it was the way they always rode into the forest, but when he got to the spot where they had been kidnapped, he couldn't tell which way the kidnappers had gone. The plume of smoke still hung in the sky, showing them the general direction, but it was a huge forest and choked with thorns and branches, shrubs and undergrowth. It was hard to see any of the paths at all. Bennett and the captain stared at the endless horizon.

'We should have brought dogs to help track,' the captain said, cross at herself for not thinking of this. 'Now we'll have to send someone back to fetch them.'

'Unless we can track the kidnappers ourselves,' Bennett suggested. 'The ground is quite muddy, and they had quite a few horses. We might be able to see hoof prints.'

He got down from his horse and looked around, but in the darkness of the forest it was impossible to see any tracks in the mud. 'I can't tell,' he said. 'I'll try over here . . .' Then, surprised, he said, 'A peppermint. It's white; I can see it in the darkness. Definitely a sweet.'

'And there's another one beyond it,' said someone.

Bennett ran forward and saw another peppermint gleaming on the forest floor just ahead, and another and then another. Quickly, surely, Prince Bennett went from one white peppermint to another, the guard following behind him as he tracked his way through the twists and turns of the impenetrable forest. 'This way,' he said quietly, and then, 'That way.' After a long time, he held up his hand to mean 'Wait!' and he turned back to the captain and said, 'They're here!'

CHAPTER SEVEN

In which Courier identifies which of his many skills saved them

The kidnappers, lulled by the warmth of the fire, did not wake, but their horses heard the palace guard horses approaching and were so irritated at having their blankets stolen, that they neighed loudly to complain of the cold. So when the captain, the guard and Bennett marched into the clearing of the forest, the kidnappers were stumbling to their feet, and sleepily demanding what all the fuss was about, and what had happened to the horses' blankets?

'You're under arrest,' the captain of the guard told them. 'Throw down your arms.'

Nobody ever refused to do what Captain Stella told them. There was a clatter as the kidnappers threw down their bows and arrows, their catapults and one rusty old sword.

'Hand over the prince and princess,' the captain demanded.

'Or vice versa,' Bennett reminded her.

'What?' she asked.

'Got to be fair,' Bennett whispered. 'Hand them over in any order. The prince or the princess. The princess or the prince. Not one before another. No one more important than the other.'

The captain was puzzled for a moment and then she turned back to the kidnappers. 'Either,' she said. 'Both. At once. And Look Smart About It.'

The chief kidnapper pointed to the shadowy hedge where Florizella and Courier had been tied to the tree. 'We want a ransom for them,' he said. 'We want a million crowns of gold.'

'Nonsense,' said Captain Stella. 'You'll hand them over right now or you'll have a million arrows through your head.'

'And besides,' Bennett pointed out, 'they're not there.'

'Not there?' the kidnapper swung round and strode over to the tree in his big villainous boots. 'Not there?'

A shower of hard peppermints on his head like hail made him look up to see Florizella and Courier looking down at him from a very high tree.

'I knew you'd save us,' Florizella said to Bennett. 'But while we were waiting, we thought we'd escape.'

'Very well done,' Bennett said.

The captain of the guard pointed the sharp end of her standard at the chief kidnapper. 'Shall it be surrender?' she asked. 'Or something much worse?'

'Just surrender please,' the kidnapper said.

All the kidnappers lined up, and the captain loaded them on to horses and sent them off to the castle dungeons, which were (as all the best dungeons always are) impenetrably deep and impossible to escape. There they

would stay until they said they were truly sorry and promised to do nothing but good in future.

The captain turned her attention to Florizella and Courier. 'Can you climb down?' she asked.

Courier looked at the ground far below him. 'You know, I don't think I can,' he admitted.

'Last time I was stuck, she let me jump into her cape,' Florizella told him. 'But we're too high for that today.' To Captain Stella she said, 'If you throw me a rope, I think I can lower him.'

The captain of the guard had a better idea. She sent up one of the guards with a pulley that they tied to a branch above Florizella and Courier's heads. Then they pulled up a great

hook, like you would see on the end of a crane, and a harness. Florizella strapped Courier into the harness, attached him to the hook, and told him to trust in team work: princes and princesses working together.

Courier stepped off his branch and the rope went taut and held his weight, then they lowered him gently to the ground. He was still so small and light that it took only one guard to hold the rope. Then they did the same thing with Florizella with two people holding the rope just to make sure that she came down slowly, without crashing into the tree.

As soon as Florizella and Courier landed, they gave Bennett a big hug and said thank you for the rescue party. They shook hands with the captain and thanked her for coming out so quickly and arresting everyone so neatly. Then they all got on their horses and rode back to the castle.

'Now that's what I call a happy ending to an adventure,' Florizella said to Prince Courier. 'And – did you see? We partly rescued ourselves, and Bennett helped us. Nobody fainted or fell asleep or cried for no reason. Nobody's heart broke and nobody was turned to stone. It's possible to have a perfectly good adventure and everyone get home with everyone helping out and doing their bit. And you were very sensible for a young prince.'

'And you were very sensible for a princess,' Courier replied. 'But the luckiest thing of all is that I'm a bit of an expert. Especially in

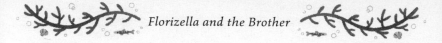

peppermints. I don't like them – especially the stripy ones. And that, after all, was what saved us.'

Florizella and the Pirates

CHAPTER ONE

*A lovely day out at the
seaside – what could
possibly go wrong?*

*P*rincess Florizella's home, the Land of the
Seven Kingdoms, and Prince Bennett's
home, the Land of Deep Lakes, are both beside
a deep unending sea that holds sea monsters,
mermaids, enormous whales, shoals of fish,
underwater mountains, drowned cities and,
of course, pirates. Just a regular fairytale sea.
The seaside towns have rocks where maidens
are sometimes tied, or pirates marooned,

unscalable cliffs and ice-cream shops and stalls selling buckets and spades. The only train in the Seven Kingdoms runs to and from the seaside so that everyone can go for a swim or a paddle on the hot days of summer and come home in the cool evening and eat fish and chips. There are no other railway lines but the coastal track, so that every train in fairytale land only goes to somewhere nice. And it's such a short journey that nobody ever asks, 'Are we there yet?' because the answer is always 'yes'.

It was just such a day when Florizella and her friend Bennett decided to take little Prince Courier to the seaside. It was the first time he had ever been to the sea, so they ordered a huge picnic from the royal kitchens and it came in a hamper so big that it had to be loaded into the luggage van of the train and travel on its own.

'What's in it?' Courier asked.

'Sandwiches,' Florizella said. 'And pies, jellies, fruit, salad, crisps, cheeses, sweets, drinks, yogurts, roast chicken and drumsticks, fish fingers and buns, hot dogs and cakes. Just the usual.'

'Have a lovely time,' the king said wistfully. 'I'd come with you myself for two pence.'

'We have work to do,' the queen reminded him.

'So we do,' the king said sadly.

Samson the royal dog, who had once been a wolf, was going with them, so the king patted him on the head, saw them all into the royal carriage and waved them off.

Florizella thought that nobody, not even a princess and two princes, should keep a carriage all to themselves. As soon as they had started along the winding track to the seaside, she opened the doors of the royal carriage so that everyone could have a seat whether they were princes and princesses or not. When they stopped at the little villages along the way people got on carrying their pigs to market, goose girls put their birds in the luggage racks, and witches made their brooms hover in the corners and sat on them, refusing to pay the full price for a seat as they had brought their own. Samson gave the brooms a long hard look and went to Bennett. Samson was not fond of magic.

Everyone was excited to be going to the

seaside for the day. The goose girls were especially nice to Florizella as there is a tradition in fairytale land of goose girls marrying royals.

'Actually, I'm not going to marry anyone,' Princess Florizella said. 'Goose girls or goat herds or anyone.'

'What about a handsome prince?' Courier asked cheekily, winking at Bennett.

'We've been through all that,' Florizella told him. 'It's a whole other story. It was written before you were even thought of.'

They got to the seaside just as it was starting to get hot. The train went along a narrow track beside the sea so people could choose where to get off. Some preferred the rock pools where they could see starfish and sea anemones, and listen to the mermaids singing. Other people preferred the sandy beach where they could build castles and moats, paddle in the sea and swim. Those who wanted to look for shells and fossils of long-ago dragons and dinosaurs got off the train at the shingle beaches. At the end of the line the train puffed uphill to the top of a narrow cliff where there was a stake with chains and a cannon with cannonballs. The train turned round on a huge turntable and was ready to make the journey home.

Florizella and Bennett thought that Courier would prefer the sandy beach for his first time at the seaside, so they got out at the station called Sandy Bay. There they spread out their picnic blanket and put up their magnificent royal tent with flags in the middle of the beach.

Courier loved the seaside. He got into his royal bathing suit at once and went for a paddle. First, he checked the lifeguard station and the flags, and when he saw that the flags were a red bar on top and a yellow bar underneath to show it was safe to swim, he went into the water, and swam where he could feel the sandy sea floor under his feet.

'A very good rule in the Prince Permit says you can swim only where you are sure to be safe,' Bennett said to Florizella. 'We princes are rather precious. We won't change that one.'

'First in and you get the best towel?' Florizella guessed.

'Oh yes, that too,' Bennett admitted.

When Courier had come out of the sea and dried off, they opened the picnic hamper.

It was a feast. There were hundreds of little sandwiches and lots of crisps. There were juices and iced water. There were cakes and ice creams and jellies, there were crisp raw vegetables and there were luscious fruits. Last of all there were perfectly cold ice lollies.

Just as they were starting to eat, a shadow fell on them, as if a cloud had covered the sun. Florizella looked up. 'Oh no!' she said. 'The Good Manner Eagles.'

'What are they?' Courier asked, reaching for a sandwich with one hand and a packet of crisps with the other.

'Freeze!' Bennett ordered. 'Courier! Don't make a move!'

Courier paused just as he was, his hand over the plate of sandwiches, his mouth open with surprise.

'Courier,' Florizella hissed in a tone that must be obeyed. 'Pass the plate to me and Bennett before you take a sandwich for yourself. Don't grab food and don't have something in each hand! And don't – whatever you do – don't talk with your mouth full!'

'Why ever not?' Courier demanded, doing exactly as he was told but in slow motion, which made him look very odd indeed.

'Up there, circling in the sky, is a Good Manner Eagle,' Florizella explained. 'It is using its remarkable vision to look down and see if we are behaving nicely, with good manners.'

'Wow!' Courier said, looking upwards and seeing the soaring bird, very big in the sky, with outspread wings and piercing yellow eyes.

'Exactly,' Bennett said. 'And if any one of the Good Manner Eagles sees anyone behaving rudely, they come swooping down like a hurricane, and tell you off.'

'Not me,' Courier said, politely handing a

plate of chicken drumsticks to Florizella. 'May
I pass you the salt?'

'Here it comes . . .' Florizella warned as the
eagle high above them closed its wings and
came diving downwards, its enormous claw
feet threateningly outstretched. It landed just
beside the three of them.

'Honestly, we've done nothing, and it's a picnic,' Florizella said at once. 'You're allowed to eat with your fingers at a picnic!'

'Informal,' Bennett agreed. 'Finger food.'

'I have been observing,' the eagle said pompously. 'As is my duty. But, anyway – it's not that. I thought you'd like to know something.'

'Always pleased to see you,' Bennett said hastily.

'Thank you for dropping in,' Florizella said. 'Would you like to join us?'

'Have you come far?' Courier asked, which is what royals always say to fill an awkward silence.

'I thought you should know that there are pirate sails on the horizon, Your Royal

Highness,' the Good Manner Eagle told Florizella – as it was her kingdom.

'No!' Bennett exclaimed. 'Really?' He turned and looked but he couldn't see anything but the endless sea sparkling in the sunshine, and every now and then the spout of water from an enormous whale going about its own business.

'Blue sails,' the eagle said. 'Hard to see. Very sneaky. Quite impolite.' He gave a leap and soared upwards into the sky again, going higher and higher until he was a little dot, and higher again until he was invisible.

Bennett jumped to his feet, shading his eyes as the sun was so dazzling. 'Florizella, Courier, can you see any ships out at sea? Pirate ships?'

Florizella and Courier stared out into the distance. Samson gave one loud warning bark, and Courier said, 'Wow! Yes! Three of them.'

How to summon a Sea Serpent (Usually, there is a better solution than this. It is very rare that the best thing to do is to call up a massive Sea Serpent. You can rely on this advice)

The two older children stared until they could quite clearly see the big square sails and just about make out the dreaded pirate flag fluttering at the back of each ship.

'I'll clear the beach,' Florizella said, running to the lifeguard chair to tell the woman who was sitting at the top. At once, the lifeguard raised a double red flag to the top of the pole and shouted through her megaphone that everyone should leave the beach as pirates were coming. Samson ran round behind everyone, herding them away, as people packed up their picnics and picked up their towels and complained that it was too early to go home and that really someone should do something about the pirates. But they all left anyway.

'Hadn't we better go, too?' Courier asked, coming up to Florizella at the lifeguard seat as the lifeguard came down the ladder and went off at a run to report.

'I can't really,' Florizella explained. 'It's my kingdom. I've got to defend it.'

'Against three full-size pirate ships?' the little prince asked. 'Just the three of us? And one of us practically born yesterday?'

'He's got a point,' Bennett said. 'What we need is a Brilliant Plan.'

'Do you have a Brilliant Plan?' Florizella asked hopefully.

'Yes,' Bennett said. 'Of course.'

There was a little pause as they waited for Bennett to explain his Brilliant Plan. Samson the wolf cub didn't wait. He went off quietly and caught the train back to the palace to tell the king. He was a very good wolf, but he had no faith in brilliant plans.

'I do have a Brilliant Plan,' Bennett said, 'but unfortunately it's got nothing to do with pirate invasion.'

'Was it really brilliant?' Courier asked loyally.

'Not now,' Florizella said sternly. 'I wonder

if the Sea Serpent might help. It doesn't like people on the cliffs or ships in the bay.'

'Then let's get it!'

'Yes,' Florizella said uncertainly. 'We should try. It's just . . . it's not easy . . . calling it up.'

'How d'you call it?' Courier asked, and then watched in surprise as Florizella did a very curious thing. She blushed: a deep rosy pink.

'You're blushing,' Bennett said, which was not helpful.

'I know,' she said, irritated. 'I can feel that I am. But I can't stop.'

'But why?' Courier asked her. 'What's the matter?'

Bennett took him by the arm to one side and said quietly, 'It's the Princess Rules. Sometimes, they're really embarrassing. Often a princess has to behave like a complete idiot. She has to be tied to a stake at the top of the cliff. It's a very pointy cliff with sea on both sides. She's not allowed to untie herself or cut the ropes. She's not allowed to climb down the cliffs or dive into the sea. She's got to wait for the Sea Serpent to come to eat her; she's not allowed to fight him, and she's only allowed to say, "Someday my prince will come." And perhaps: "Oh! Save Me."'

Courier snorted with giggles, but Bennett, one eye on Florizella, who was listening to him explain and not looking very helpless at all, gave him a little nudge. 'Shush. She doesn't like it.'

'OK, OK,' said Courier. 'So what happens then?'

'Then a prince comes, and he fights the Sea Serpent (very bravely) and he wins, and frees the princess, and marries her. Florizella just hates that story.'

'Because the princess does nothing?' Courier asked, knowing that his sister was a girl who liked to get things done, and do them for herself.

Florizella finally spoke through her teeth. 'And also because of what the princess has to wear.'

'What's that?'

'Long dress: pink,' Bennett listed. 'Tall hat with pink veil. Hair long, preferably in ringlets or curls. Arms tied behind back. Bare feet or teeny-tiny pink silk slippers, quite useless for running away. Pink varnish on her toenails. No weapons, not even a hidden dagger, no armour, no fighting. No Brilliant Plan.'

'And what she has to say,' prompted Florizella.

'"Help help,"' Bennett recited. '"Oh! Oh! If only a handsome prince would come and save me."'

'Really, that's OK,' Courier reassured Florizella. 'It's just acting a part. It's just saying words. Anybody could do it.'

'You think so?' Florizella said irritably. 'You do it, then.'

'OK,' Courier agreed easily. 'I will.'

The two of them looked at him.

'Wouldn't you hate it?' Florizella said. 'Acting helpless and waiting for a sea monster, while a prince gets all the adventure, and you are either a bride or lunch?'

'It's quite a brave thing to do really,' Courier pointed out. 'You save the kingdom from the pirates. You choose it for yourself. And I'd love to wear a pink dress.'

'Why?' Florizella was amazed.

'Why not? I like pink. I like dresses, especially long ones, especially really swishy ones. Why not?'

'It might work,' Bennett said thoughtfully. 'But we'd have to be sure that we rescued him, Florizella. Your mum and dad will go mad if they find out that we've taken him to the seaside and got him eaten. They'll go bonkers if we don't bring him back safely. Especially as he's a new baby, and he's their only— ' Bennett swallowed the last word he was going to say.

'Boy,' Florizella said, finishing his sentence.

'He's their only boy. I know. But look – there will be two of us to fight the Sea Serpent, instead of one. Courier isn't bound by the Princess Rules, so he can untie his ropes and join in. He's not bound by the Princess Rules so he can be brave, and he can fight. We ought to win, and then we can make the Sea Serpent help us with the pirates.'

'It's not really a Brilliant Plan,' Bennett said sadly. 'It's too complicated.'

'It's the only one we've got.'

CHAPTER THREE

*In which we see how pirates
can ruin a lovely day out, and —
as well! — there is a Sea Serpent*

A few hours later, the pirate ships were still far out at sea, and the three royals had hauled the picnic hamper up the steep cliffs. They were at the top, unpacking the special box that was kept at the narrow pointy end of the cliff for the princess sacrifice. It was labelled very clearly.

KEEP OUT.
PRINCESS SACRIFICE KIT.
USE ONLY IN AN EMERGENCY.
GOOD LUCK, YOUR ROYAL HIGHNESS!
(PLEASE DO NOT REUSE BLOODSTAINED DRESSES.)

The princess stake, stuck like a lamp post on the narrow clifftop, was still there from the last time a princess had been offered to the Sea Serpent.

'Do you know any of the sacrifices?' Courier asked curiously as they dressed him in the special doomed gown and combed his curly blond hair under the tall pink hat.

'My mum, the queen,' Florizella said. 'My dad rescued her, and they married and lived happily ever after. Look, she carved her initials here.'

Courier looked at all the initials of princesses

carved on the stake. Every now and then there was a gap as if a girl had failed to write her name. 'What about her?' he asked. 'She just seems to have started a C.'

'Sweet Princess Claire,' Florizella said.

'Eaten?' Courier started to look rather nervous.

'The clue's in the name,' Bennett told him. '*Sweet* Princess Claire. Gone in a moment. Like a jellybaby. See this one?

'G?'

'Chewy Princess Giselle,' Florizella said. 'She was lucky – he spat her out. Too tough. But all the rest of the gaps on the stake are princesses who were eaten so quickly that they didn't even have time to carve their name. That's the thing – if you rely on a prince to save you, and he doesn't get here in time, then it's one for the Sea Serpent.'

Courier turned a little pale as they tied him up to the stake.

'But we'll be sure to rescue you, because we're right here, right now,' Bennett reassured him. 'And besides, you're a prince, not a princess.'

'Can a Sea Serpent tell the difference?' Courier asked.

'Well, there isn't much difference,' Florizella agreed. 'A princess is just a prince with more SSs.'

'What are the SSs for?'

'Sea Serpent,' said Bennett.

Florizella laughed. 'Yes, that's a good one—'

'No, I mean it . . . SEA SERPENT!'

And out of the deep blue water uncoiled an enormous shiny green Sea Serpent with a neck as tall as the steep cliffs, and a body with miles of scaly humps. It had a head like a huge dragon, beautiful deep blue eyes, and flaring gills. With a mouth like an alligator, its jaws yawned wide towards Courier as he stood in his beautiful pink dress with his pink tall hat until he shook so much that his veil trembled and he looked just like a terrified princess about to be eaten in a fairy tale.

'Wow,' said Florizella, very interested. 'I had no idea it was that big.'

'Your mum must be absolutely hardcore,' said Bennett, 'to be tied up and wait for this to come for her.'

'She is,' Florizella said. 'She really is.'

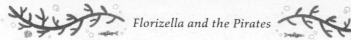 

'Oh!' said Courier in a high little voice. 'Help, help! Oh! If only a handsome prince would come and rescue me.'

'And she was here for three days,' Florizella pointed out, watching the Sea Serpent as it reared over the helpless prince.

'Some day my prince will come!' Courier bellowed.

'Why so long?' Bennett asked.

'My dad was late,' Florizella said. 'She's never forgiven him.'

Courier looked across at Florizella and Bennett. 'Help, help,' Courier shrieked at the top of his voice. 'Oh! If only a handsome prince would come and rescue me! Now! RIGHT NOW! And concentrate! On what we are supposed to be doing!'

'Gosh!' Bennett said. 'Sorry! Yes!'

'Be right with you, Courier!' Florizella said. 'Draw swords!'

Bennett and Florizella drew their swords and jumped out either side of Courier and faced the Sea Serpent.

'Not fair! Not fair!' the creature said irritably. 'Two to one isn't fair!'

'We don't want to fight you,' Florizella explained. 'We just wanted to call you because we need your help.'

'Why didn't you ring the bell, then?'

Halfway down the cliffs, far too steep to climb, was a doorbell. Above it was a sign that read:

No CALLERS. No JUNK MAIL.

Below it was a sign that read:

> No visitors.
> No after-lunch mourners.

Below that was a sign that read:

> I'M A SEA SERPENT;
> IT IS MY NATURE TO EAT PRINCESSES.
> YOU DON'T WANT ME TO DENY MY NATURE, DO YOU?
> **I HAVE TO EXPRESS MYSELF!**

'I didn't know you had a doorbell,' Florizella apologised. 'Anyway, I wouldn't have been able to climb down to it, I don't think. Or up. The cliffs *are* called the Unscalable Cliffs. That means nobody can scale them. "Scale" means climb.'

'Exactly! Because I don't want anyone climbing down and ringing it,' the Sea Serpent said crossly.

'How many times do you think people would ring and run away? Ho, ho, very funny, I don't think.'

'What about when people come to, er . . . visit?' Bennett asked. 'Friends.'

'I don't have any friends,' the Sea Serpent said. 'I don't have a friendly nature.'

'I'm sure you do,' Florizella urged, trying to be pleasant.

'I don't want a friendly nature.'

'But *we* want to be your friends. And we really need your help.'

The Sea Serpent put its strangely beautiful head on one side and looked at Florizella, as if considering if she might make a good friend. Or perhaps it was wondering if she would make a good lunch. 'No,' it said after a moment's thought. 'All I really like are enemies. And dinner.'

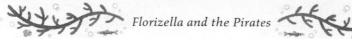 

'We've got enemies for you!' Courier cried out. 'Great enemies! Coming this way.'

The Sea Serpent looked at him crossly. 'Don't talk,' it said. 'It's bad manners to talk when you're a mouthful.'

'You can't have him for lunch,' Florizella said quickly. 'And we really do have enemies for you.'

The Sea Serpent looked closely at her. 'Aren't you a princess? Under all the dirt?'

'Yes,' Florizella said. 'I am. But I don't obey the Princess Rules. Nobody eats me for lunch.'

'Very irregular,' the Sea Serpent said quietly to itself.

'And we really do have enemies for you,' Bennett interrupted. 'Bad enemies. How do you feel about pirates?'

'I hate them!' the Sea Serpent announced. 'So noisy! So chewy, far too salty!'

'Well, there are three ships of pirates and they're coming this way!' Florizella told it. 'And we hoped you would help us arrest them.'

'I'll arrest them if I can eat them,' the Sea Serpent offered. 'Not otherwise. If I can't eat them, I'll eat this one.' It smiled at Courier in a way that was not very nice to see. It licked its lips with its long, winding tongue.

'All right,' Bennett said. To Florizella he whispered, 'Best we can do.'

'I don't think it's quite the best for me,' Courier said reproachfully. He was still tied to the princess stake in the beautiful pink gown with the tall princess hat and veil. But he didn't look happy. Sometimes, even a great dress doesn't help that much.

'Stand to!' Florizella said. 'Pirates approaching!' She turned to the Sea Serpent. 'Does the cannon fire?'

'Perfectly,' the Sea Serpent said, pointing with its long noble nose to the cannon on the little platform over the sea. 'Why don't you bombard them with cannonballs and, when they halt, order them away? Then, if they come on, I'll wrap them in my coils and drown them.'

'Hang on,' Bennett said. 'They've got to be arrested, not drowned on sight. This has got to be fair.'

The Sea Serpent gave a little shudder that made its scales rustle. 'I don't really care about fair,' it said. 'Not when it's me with the advantage.'

'Looks like you always have the advantage,' Courier said crossly from where he was still tied up. He did not like the Sea Serpent's attitude – he did not like it one bit.

'It's just the Allowance,' the Sea Serpent explained. 'Princesses get eaten, princes get to fight, and Sea Serpents get an Allowance. Why should anything ever change?'

'I don't want them to drown,' Florizella said. 'Some of them might not be pirates at all but prisoners. Some of them might be sorry. Some of them might be children and not know of any other life but the pirate way. Who knows? We've got to stop them and arrest them and talk to them.'

The Sea Serpent looked blank. 'No, I'm not

following you there. Why don't I just eat them?'

'Do you eat picnic?' Courier suddenly asked.

The Sea Serpent turned to him. 'Princesses. Not picnic.'

'It's still a P,' Courier said. 'And very tasty. And never tough. There's never anything tough in a picnic.'

Bennett threw back the lid of the picnic hamper and the Sea Serpent saw all the delicious things that Florizella had brought from the palace. Ham sandwiches and crisps, cakes and jellies, raspberries and muffins, lemonade and cold chicken. The Sea Serpent's beautiful blue eyes sparkled, and it looked yearningly from the food to Courier, as if it were trying to choose. 'PICNIC,' it said. 'Never seen a picnic before. Perhaps better than a princess.'

'Much better,' Courier said. 'And it comes in a hamper. And it doesn't have parents. Nobody comes round to complain after it's been eaten. There aren't any mourners or flowers to bother you. Let's stop the pirates first, and then we can all eat the picnic.'

The Sea Serpent put its head on one side to think, but its blue eyes never left the picnic hamper.

'So you can untie me now,' Courier said quietly to Bennett.

'You know, I think it's going to be OK,' Bennett whispered to Florizella.

'I think it is . . .' she replied. 'We're going to have to load the cannon . . .'

'Would you two please remember me and untie me now!' Courier snapped.

CHAPTER FOUR

*In which everyone learns
the meaning of the interesting
word 'recoil'*

lorizella got the old cannon ready for firing as Bennett untied Courier and the Sea Serpent watched the pirates getting steadily closer. Florizella cleaned out the deep barrel of the cannon with a mop on a long handle and then unfolded the cannon firing instructions from the box.

Like all instructions, they made no sense at all at first. She had to read and reread them,

and then she had to get all the bits lined up.
Florizella said what everyone says when they
first look at instructions. 'There must be a part
missing!'

'It's all there,' the Sea Serpent said irritably.
'You just have to do everything in the right
order. You have to follow the instructions, and
mind the recoil.'

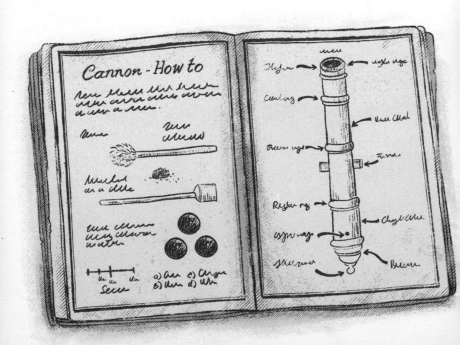

'"Take gunpowder bag and ram it gently down the barrel of the cannon,"' Bennett read out helpfully. 'Gently!' he shouted as Florizella shoved it in. 'This stuff explodes!'

'It's supposed to explode!' she pointed out. 'It's gunpowder.'

'It's supposed to explode when you fire it! Not when you're loading it because you're smashing it about.'

'Hurry up,' Courier said. 'They're coming closer.'

'"Take some wadding,"' Bennett said, reading the instructions.

'Whatting?' Florizella asked.

'Wadding, like paper or cloth, and you push it in after the gunpowder but before the cannonball, so the cannonball doesn't squash the gunpowder, and make it explode in the barrel.'

'There's none here,' Florizella said, looking into the box. 'Nothing.'

'They're coming into range,' Courier warned them. 'You've got to hurry.'

'Your gown, Courier!' Florizella said. 'That'd be perfect.'

With only a second's hesitation Courier ripped off his princess gown, bundled it into a cushion shape and Florizella gently pushed it into the barrel of the cannon with the handle of her mop. Courier helped, wearing only his high hat and his bathing shorts.

'I must say, you do have a very individual fashion style,' the Sea Serpent remarked, as the three royals rolled the cannon to the front edge

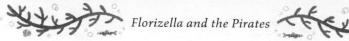
of the platform that stretched out over the sea. Bennett pricked the gunpowder bag through the little hole in the top of the cannon, and Florizella poked in the piece of special string that was the fuse so it touched the gunpowder and then she got the matches ready.

'Says here, "Stand clear of the recoil,"' Florizella read. 'What does that mean?'

'Oh! Let me light it! Do let me!' begged Courier.

Florizella hesitated.

'He was very brave about being sacrificed,' Bennett reminded her.

'Go on, then.' Florizella handed the matches and the fuse to the little boy. 'But what is recoil?'

'Take aim!' Bennett said, standing right

behind the cannon in order to aim, and looking down the long barrel.

'And FIRE!' Florizella said, standing behind him to check that he was right.

Courier, immediately behind the gun, touched the match to the fuse. The flame ran rapidly along the fuse and, *BANG*, there was an enormous explosion. The cannonball arched from the mouth of the gun over the Sea Serpent's head into the air and – *SPLAT* – hit the water just in front of the first pirate ship, swamping them and half drowning the other ships with a massive wave.

'Good shot,' cried the Sea Serpent, 'oh, jolly good shot!' as the cannon recoiled, flying backwards from the explosion and bouncing the three royal children backwards off the

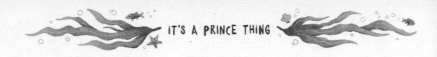

incredibly high cliff and down with a huge splash into the sea below.

Bennett was first up, breaking the water and bobbing in the waves, coughing. 'What was that?' he spluttered. 'Did they fire back? One minute I was there, thinking we had won, and the next moment I'm underwater and nearly drowned.'

Florizella came up beside him, treading water. 'So that's what it means,' she said. 'I did wonder.'

'What?'

'The instructions. They said, "Stand clear of the recoil". I think "recoil" means when the gun rolls back after firing. We didn't stand clear. We were right behind it.'

'Now you say!' Bennett said crossly, starting to swim towards the distant shore.

'I said before,' Florizella said. 'I just didn't realise that the instructions meant what they said so very much.'

'I didn't hear you.'

'I definitely said it,' she said irritably, swimming after him.

'If it's a warning, you should say it really loud.'

'It was loud enough. Because I didn't know what it meant anyway. And you didn't know what it meant. So it could have been ten times louder and it would have made no difference . . .'

This could have gone on all day when suddenly Florizella realised the most terrible thing.

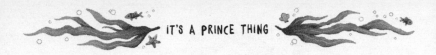

'Where's Courier?' she said, turning round and treading water. Then she said again, in a much more frightened voice: 'Bennett! Where is Courier?'

CHAPTER FIVE

In which Florizella fears that she only had a baby brother for four days

*B*ennett dived and Florizella dived too. They went down and down, deep into the water to see if they could find Courier trapped in the weeds, or perhaps with his foot caught by a giant clam. Worse still, he could have been kidnapped by mermaids, or stampeded by seahorses, or turned into a whelk by a water witch, or suffered any of the many accidents that happen to unfortunate princes underwater. But there was no trace of him, and though they caught two dolphins and rode them around, they couldn't see him anywhere.

'And the pirates will still be coming to shore,' Bennett reminded her, bobbing up in the waves. 'We've got to save the kingdom.'

'You go and stop the pirates; I'll go on looking for Courier,' Florizella said. She was very frightened. 'He's my little brother – I should never have put him in any danger.'

Bennett didn't know what was best. 'I don't want to leave you here. You know what happens in fairy tales: as soon as someone leaves the princess, something terrible happens to her.'

'It's happened already,' Florizella said grimly. 'What could be worse than this? You

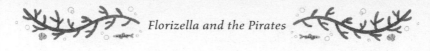

go and get rid of the pirates. Then come back here. And bring the Sea Serpent with you. It should be able to find Courier, even if we can't.'

Bennett nodded and swam to shore as Florizella dived down and swam around searching. Then she dived – again and again.

On the clifftop, the Sea Serpent was waiting irritably, as Bennett reappeared, panting and very wet, having swum to the shore and run beside the train track to the top of the cliff.

'Where did you go?' the Sea Serpent asked. 'One minute you were there, and the next you were gone.'

'The cannon recoil hit us and sent us over the edge and into the sea,' Bennett explained.

'But now Courier is missing, and Florizella is hunting for him. As soon as we have sorted out the pirates, you have to come and find him.'

'I?' said the Sea Serpent. 'I find him? I'm not really interested in finding him. Unless it's "finders eaters", of course.'

'You have to help us,' Bennett said earnestly. 'We have to find him. And anyway, there's no picnic for anyone until we do.'

The Sea Serpent sighed, as if Bennett was being very unreasonable. 'Well, do you want to warn these pirates? The ships are all hove to, and they're all shouting at each other.'

'They're what?'

'Stopped where they are,' the Sea Serpent explained.

'Oh, all right. Can I signal to them from here?'

'Why don't you ride behind my gills? We could go out to them and we would look – I say it myself – spectacular.'

'I could ride on your neck?' Bennett was still worried for Courier. But this was pretty awesome.

In answer, the Sea Serpent bowed its great head and Bennett slung his leg over the great scaly neck and looked down the long noble nose.

'You may hold my ears for balance,' the Sea Serpent said graciously. Bennett, feeling that this was a little bit too intimate, got a good grip and looked out to sea where he could see the three pirate ships, quite close to the bay, dropping their sails and not sure what to do.

'Ready?' the Sea Serpent asked.

'Get set, go!' Bennett said, like he was starting a wonderful race.

'I was going anyway,' the Sea Serpent remarked, and it swooshed through the water towards the pirate ship so fast that they left a great bow wave behind them, like a dark blue V.

'Hold tight,' it said as it reared up high over the first ship and then dived into the sea beside it. Then it came up beside the second ship, jumped over that and into the sea, and the same to the third, so that when it came up and looked back all three pirate ships were held tight in the Sea Serpent's scaly green coils. They couldn't go forwards or backwards, but they could definitely go down.

'Now you can tell them,' the Sea Serpent said with confidence. 'And I think you'll find they won't argue.'

'Pirates!' Bennett yelled from his wonderful place on the Sea Serpent's high head. 'You are under arrest. You are to come with me to the Queasy Quays, where no one sets sail but the seasick, and wait there till the king and queen of the Seven Kingdoms give their orders.'

The chief of pirates, a fearsome woman called Five Fathom Frieda, would have argued, but she caught the beautiful blue gaze of the Sea Serpent and she said quietly, and a bit sulkily, 'Or what?'

'Or I will squeeze,' the Sea Serpent said quietly. 'Believe me, you don't want to be squeezed.'

Five-Fathom Frieda shook her head. She had deep blue ringlets and they bobbed hard when she shook her head. She was so very sure that she didn't want to be squeezed.

'The Sea Serpent will take you into the Queasy Quays,' Bennett said. 'And the king and queen and I and the Princess Florizella and Prince Courier will meet you there.'

He very much hoped that Florizella and Courier *would* meet them there, but there was no point in telling the pirates that he'd lost two of the heroic three royals. To the Sea Serpent he said quietly in its big green ear, 'Actually, could you drop me off behind the cliff to look for Courier and Florizella?'

CHAPTER SIX

It is a little late to talk about good manners. But here are the Good Manner Eagles

Meanwhile, Florizella had been swimming in wider and wider and wider circles, looking down into the water, diving down when she caught sight of anything, hoping that she would see Courier somewhere on the seabed, or in the sea. But there was no sign of him. Florizella kept bobbing up out of the water to take a breath and shout, "Courier!", but there really was no sign of him at all.

She asked fish; she asked bobbing octopi who shrugged their many shoulders – no one had seen him. Florizella was more frightened for her little brother than she had ever been in her whole life. More frightened than when she had met the dragon, or the wolves, or the giant or the kidnappers. Finally, she climbed out of the sea to the foot of the Unscalable Cliffs and there she found Bennett dismounting from the Sea Serpent, which had three pirate ships wrapped in its snaky coils.

'Can't find him,' was all she said. 'I've been looking and looking.'

It was such dreadful news that Bennett went quite white. 'I was certain he'd turn up. Probably talking. Full of himself.'

Florizella shook her head. 'This is dreadful,' she said. 'Worse than dreadful. And I keep thinking . . .' Her voice got all croaky and she stopped to sniff.

'You can cry,' Bennett offered. 'Girls and boys can cry when they need to.'

'I'm not being a cry baby?' Florizella checked.

'Not when it's important,' he assured her.

Two tears rolled down Florizella's cheeks at the thought of her lost brother. 'How ever am I going to tell Mum and Dad?' Florizella whispered.

And that was when they heard the royal trumpets from the Queasy Quays, and the sky over their head went dark as two Good Manner Eagles swooped down.

'We're not late!' Florizella and Bennett

both shouted. But the claws of both huge birds had fastened into their belts and hauled them off the beach and up into the sky.

'Punctuality,' said one bird.

'Is the politeness of princes,' completed the other.

'We weren't late; we're not even expected!' Florizella explained.

'Definitely expected,' said one eagle.

'Can't be late for the king,' said the other.

'Nothing more important than good manners!' they said together in a terribly smug chorus. 'That's what we say!'

'That's what you always say,' Florizella complained. 'And you swoop down and grab me, and half the time I didn't even have to go! But you never listen to me!'

The two royals, dangling helplessly from the Good Manner Eagles' claws, were flown to the Queasy Quays and dropped gently in a wet heap before Florizella's mother and father. Samson went up to them both and sniffed them over. He was glad to see them. He had run to fetch help the moment Bennett had said he had a Brilliant Plan. Samson the wolf thought that help was better than a Brilliant Plan, and this time he was right.

'Mum, it's about Courier . . .' Florizella started at once.

'Isn't he clever?' her mother said. 'An island of his own! A whole new kingdom!'

'No, we lost—' Florizella started, and then went quiet when Bennett leaned gently but warningly against her.

'Where is he?' Bennett asked. 'Our very clever Prince Courier?'

'There!' said the queen, stepping back and pointing into the harbour. And there was the Sea Serpent, looking very pleased with itself with three pirate ships wound up in its infinite coils. Beyond it, further out to sea, there was Courier, standing on a small rounded black island, and holding the flag of the Seven Kingdoms to claim the territory.

CHAPTER SEVEN

In which Courier discovers an unknown island

'Y-you're OK?' Florizella stammered. She could hardly believe her eyes. 'Courier? You're all right?'

Courier grinned at her. 'Fell into the sea, swam around for a bit, landed on this island,' he said. 'Pretty good, eh? For a first solo adventure.'

'That's m'boy!' said the king proudly.

'Hmm, yes,' said Florizella. 'But before we

get on to how clever Prince Courier is, what are we going to do about the pirates?'

The king and the queen had a brief chat. 'We're going to let them go, if they promise not to come near the Land of the Seven Kingdoms again,' the king said finally. 'They have said they are sorry.'

'Extremely sorry,' said Five-Fathom Frieda with an eye on the Sea Serpent coils that squeezed just a little, like a gentle hint, and made her ship's timbers crack and creak. 'Ready to sail away the moment we're released, my hearties.'

'"Your Majesties" is the more usual way of addressing us,' the queen said quietly as the Good Manner Eagles nodded and looked down their beaks.

'So rude!' one whispered to the other.

'Ready to sail away the moment we're released, Your Majesties,' Five-Fathom Frieda corrected herself.

'And the Sea Serpent?' Bennett asked. 'The Sea Serpent has been very helpful.'

'Indispensable,' the Sea Serpent claimed. It smiled at the queen, who gave it a long, hard look, as if neither of them had forgotten the three days when they waited for the king to rescue her.

'The Sea Serpent is going to guard the coast forever,' the queen said. 'And we're going to give it a medal.'

'And a picnic every summer,' the Sea Serpent reminded them all.

'And now Prince Courier can name his

island and claim it for the kingdom,' the king said. 'Courierland sounds good. *Undootedly!*'

Bennett whispered in Florizella's ear. 'Florizella – don't you think there is something a bit funny about Courierland?'

'Like it's moving slightly?' Florizella said. 'Sort of bobbing.'

'It must have moved. It must have moved a long way. We fell off the Unscalable Cliffs and Courier must have climbed ashore near there. But now here we are at the Queasy Quays, right round the cliffs on the other side. It's moved a lot. It's practically sailed.'

'There aren't any trees on that island,' Florizella observed. 'Not even grass.'

'No sand. Just black rock.'

'I name this island . . .' Prince Courier lifted

the royal standard to stick it into the ground of
his new island.

'No!' yelled Bennett, suddenly realising what the island must be.

'Stop!' shouted Florizella.

But they were too late. As Courier plunged the royal standard into what he thought was earth beneath his feet, an enormous whale, which had been sleeping very sweetly and dreaming interesting dreams, suddenly felt a piercing blow in its head. In shock it let out a plume of water from its blowhole, and dived deep.

Whooosh! A great wave swept Courier off the whale's back, down to the depths of the ocean and then washed him back up again on to the quayside where Bennett and Florizella quickly grabbed him so that he couldn't be swept back into the sea again. All the pirate ships bounced up and down in the swirling seas. The whale went down to the very depths of the ocean, and then came up again to blow a huge indignant plume of water into the sky.

'What Was That?' it bellowed in an enormously deep loud voice.

'An accident,' Florizella said quickly. 'Very unfortunate. My little brother mistook you for an island.'

'HOW?' the whale bellowed. 'IS HE AN IDIOT?'

'Well . . .' Florizella started.

'You're so very big,' Bennett said. The whale looked furious, so Bennett carried right on. 'And so very handsome. Not a barnacle on you. He thought you were an island of beautiful black marble.'

The whale let out a little satisfied spout. 'Go on,' he said. 'He didn't!'

'He did,' Florizella joined in. 'I thought you were a jet mountain when I first saw you. I've never seen anything like you before. Huge, black and shining, quite beautiful.'

'Silly,' the whale said, smiling now. 'Well, I hope the little minnow isn't hurt?'

'No, I'm fine,' Courier said, ignoring being called a little minnow, in order not to upset the whale again. 'I hope I didn't hurt you with the flag?'

'No, it was just a surprise,' the whale said. 'I'll be going now.' And he spouted water again and sank to the bottom of the ocean.

'Really ought to bow before you go,' said one

of the Good Manner Eagles, but the whale was already gone.

'Courier!' the queen said. 'You must be more careful! Fancy climbing on to a whale! And whatever were you doing that far out to sea?'

'It was the recoil from the cannon—' Courier started to say, but Bennett and Florizella both leaned on him from each side, so that he could say no more.

'Your Majesty, would you . . .'

'Mummy Queen, I'm terribly . . .'

'Start the picnic for the Sea Serpent?'

'Hungry.'

The queen laughed at the two of them. 'Yes,' she said. 'And the pirates can have a picnic before they go too.'

So the king and queen, the pirates from the

three pirate ships, the Sea Serpent, Princess Florizella, Prince Bennett and Prince Courier all had a delicious picnic on the Queasy Quays.

Afterwards, Florizella, doing her job as a big sister, teaching Courier the things he needed to know as a prince of the Seven Kingdoms, took him to one side. 'See?' she said. 'We've had a lovely day out at the seaside and nobody was drowned, or eaten by Sea Serpents, or invaded by pirates. Just a nice day out and a picnic, and you learned to swim safely in the sea, as a young prince should.'

'And you learned the meaning of the word "recoil",' Courier replied. 'So we have both learned something today, which is – after all – the main thing.'

Florizella and
the Woolly Mammoth

CHAPTER ONE

In which Courier becomes an inventor

'Where's Courier?' Bennett asked Florizella, as they were walking towards the stables.

'I don't know,' Florizella said. 'Growing somewhere, I suppose. He's always growing, that boy. Probably deciding what the main thing is. He likes to decide things.'

'I'm here!' came a squawk from one of the stables and the two royals looked over the stable door.

There was a strange contraption in the stable, a bit like a bicycle but with four wheels. A bit like a narrow cart but with no room to load any goods, just a high seat on a box. Courier was working underneath it so they could only see his sticking-out feet.

'What's that?' Bennett asked.

Courier emerged, smiling. 'It's a car,' he said surprisingly. 'I've invented a car.'

They were stunned.

'What's a car?' Bennett asked.

'Why?' Florizella demanded.

Courier came out from under the car and leaned on the stable door. 'Good questions,' he said. 'As it happens, I'm a bit of an expert. A car is a way of travelling much faster than a horse. And you can go wherever you want.'

'You can't go exactly wherever you want,' Florizella pointed out. 'You have to go where the roads go. Unlike horses. Horses really can go anywhere.'

'Yes, we'll have to build more roads,' Courier agreed. 'Thousands of them. Millions. Everyone has to have a road to their garage.'

'What's a garage?' Bennett asked, while Florizella said nothing, thinking about millions of roads all around the Seven Kingdoms.

'A house for a car,' Courier explained. 'We'll have to build millions—'

'Hang on a minute,' Florizella interrupted him. 'You've invented a way of carrying people around – which is great – but each car has to have its own road and its own garage? Isn't this a bit . . . inconvenient?'

'You can get them in all different colours,' Courier said, as if that made all the difference. 'We'll sell new ones every year. And they will all have different names.'

'Why?' Bennett asked. 'Do they answer to their names?'

'No,' Courier said. 'It's just to make sure that people keep buying the new ones and dumping the old ones.'

'Dumping them?' Bennett asked.

'Yes, we'll have to build massive car dumps too.'

'But where is everyone going to go in their thousands of cars?' Florizella asked.

Courier thought for a moment. 'They'll have to drive to work,' he said. 'They're going to need to work a lot more to earn more

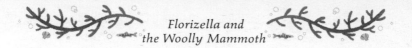

money to buy all these new cars.'

'And what does the car do, while they're at work?'

'It waits for them. In a car park. That reminds me – we're going to need thousands of car parks too.'

'So, the car drives from the garage to the car park, waits and comes home again?' Bennett double-checked.

'Yes,' Courier said firmly, but he wasn't feeling so certain now. 'Of course, if everyone is going to the same place, we could perhaps connect one car after another and they could all go together. That would probably be better.'

'Then it would be a train,' Florizella pointed out.

'But this is the future!' Courier exclaimed.

'Look! I'll show you.' He opened up the stable door and wheeled out his device: the car. He opened the bonnet and tightened some screws then he got on to the box, and started the engine. There was a mighty roar and a cloud of smoke billowed out of the back of the engine.

'What's that?' Bennett asked, waving away the stinking cloud.

'Exhaust fumes,' Courier choked. 'It's a bit of a problem, I know. But if there's a good breeze it will just blow the dirty air into the next-door kingdom.'

'That's my kingdom,' Bennett said mildly.
'So, I don't think that's a good idea.'

'The engine is the best bit!' Courier said.
'Worth a bit of smoke. Climb on.'

The two older children climbed on Courier's
brilliant invention and drove slowly out of the
royal palace and down the hill. It was market
day in the town and all the stalls were laid out in
the town square, with people walking around
and talking and buying. The horse-drawn
wagons were going slowly round the square so
Courier had to queue up behind them.

'How fast does it go?' Bennett asked.

'Incredibly fast,' Courier said happily.

'How fast are we going now?'

'About two miles an hour,' Courier admitted.
'That's the trouble. There are too many people. I

won't allow anyone on the new roads: just cars.'

'The cars get roads all to themselves?' Florizella asked. 'Where do the people and horses go?'

'They'll probably have to stay at home,' Courier said thoughtfully. 'They won't want to be on the noisy, dirty roads with cars speeding by really fast. Hang on a minute, I have to refuel.'

He pulled over to the side of the road and took out a chest of treasure from under one of the seats.

'What fuel does it use?' Florizella asked.

'Diamonds,' he said. 'Isn't that brilliant?'

'Isn't that expensive?' Bennett asked. 'And won't they run out?'

'Well, yes, but the whole point of the car is

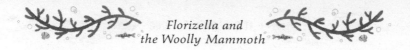

that people make money from the drivers.'

'The thing is,' Florizella said, 'this is fairytale land and we don't want to cover it with tarmac just for cars and have people work extra hours to buy cars that can't take them anywhere, and which cost a fortune to fuel, so that a few people – the owners of the car factories – get really rich, and everyone else gets poor buying cars and buying the fuel.'

'But don't you think this is going to make people really happy?' Courier demanded, waving at his car, which could go no faster than the slowest person on the road, and which burned up diamonds that could never be replaced, which poured out dirty smoke and came in many different colours and had many different names so people would be constantly worrying about whether they should get a new one.

'Is it making you happy?'

'Well, it was,' Courier said sulkily. 'But now I'm rather going off my brilliant invention. It looked great at first, but I don't like it so much now. In fact, I wish I'd never thought of it at all.'

CHAPTER TWO

In which Courier discovers it is harder to get rid of cars than invent them

't's going to be all right. This is fairytale land,' Florizella assured Courier. 'We can get the royal enchanter to uninvent your car. We can have the future we want.'

So the three children parked Courier's brilliant invention, the car, at the side of a grassy track that was bordered with wild flowers, and busy with bees.

'How do we get the royal enchanter to come

and uninvent it?' Courier asked. 'Should I invent a telephone?'

'No!' Bennett and Florizella said together.

'That's enough inventions for one day,' Florizella told him. 'You get a royal enchanter by wishing for one. They know when they're wanted.'

The three of them joined hands, closed their eyes and wished very earnestly that an enchanter would come and help them out with Courier's inconvenient invention. There was a rumble like thunder and a crack of lightning, and not one, not two, but three enchanters suddenly appeared in the middle of the hand-clasped children.

'Oh!' Florizella said. 'Three of you.'

'Three wishes,' the royal enchanter of the Seven Kingdoms told her severely. 'That's a

good number for wishes, but usually you do one after another.' He smiled and started his only enchanter joke. 'And d'you know what number three wish should be?'

'Yes,' Florizella said.

'You do? How do you know? This is an enchanter joke.'

'Number-three wish should be for three more wishes,' Florizella said. He had told her the wishing joke something like three million times.

'That's right!' He drew his purple robe round him and straightened his tall purple enchanter hat. 'Ha, ha, ha. Very funny. My little joke.'

'Mine too,' said the other two.

'I see there are three of you,' the enchanter

of the Seven Kingdoms said. 'That explains the triplicate summons.'

'Triplicate?' Courier asked, interested.

'Three of them,' Bennett explained. To his own enchanter from the Land of Deep Lakes, who was wearing a dark greeny-blue robe, he said, 'Good morning, Sir. Thank you for coming.'

'If he means three, why doesn't he just say three?' Courier persisted. The third enchanter tapped him on the shoulder with his long golden wand, which matched his yellow and orange swirly robe. 'Where did you come from?' Courier asked.

'Just passing,' the orange-coloured enchanter said. 'And someone wished for me.'

'In triplicate!' Courier agreed. He loved new

words. 'Sorry about that. It's because there were three of us wishing at once.'

'But what did you want us to do?' the orange enchanter asked.

'I've got this this brilliant invention.' Courier took the enchanter by the corner of his sleeve and led him to the car. 'The thing is, it's not such a good idea as I'd first thought. I'd like you to uninvent it.'

'What does it run on?' the enchanter asked, taking a look at the engine.

Courier took hold of the enchanter's enormously long snowy beard to direct his attention to the fuel tank. 'That's part of the trouble,' he said. 'Diamonds.'

'Must make it very expensive,' Bennett's enchanter chimed in. 'It would have been better to run it on magic.'

'Then it wouldn't have been a car,' Courier explained. 'It could have been a coach made from a pumpkin and drawn by rats once you start getting magic into it. I wanted something a bit more normal.'

'There's nothing normal about the only car in the entire world that runs on diamonds,' Florizella's enchanter pointed out. He held his sleeves and his beard out of the way, as if he feared Courier would lay hold of him, and he leaned forward to have a good look at the car.

'If it carried more people and didn't throw out dirty smoke it would be OK,' he said.

'Then it would be a train,' Florizella said patiently, feeling that she had said this once before.

'What about a fuel like rain?' Bennett's enchanter suggested. 'That's practically free.'

'Or snow?' said the bright orange enchanter. 'Snow would be great. We could magic up a great iceberg and people could just chip off a chunk, pop it in the fuel tank, and away they would go, watering the verge as they drove along. Nice.'

'That is quite nice,' said Florizella's enchanter. 'But where would you get an iceberg from? In midsummer?'

'The snowy north?'

'The snowy south?' the other enchanters suggested together. 'From the glaciers and mountains? What about the Snow Queen? She must have some to spare.'

'I thought you might just uninvent the car?' Florizella asked. 'Return it to a little idea in my little brother's little brain – something that just flies through for a moment and doesn't stop? Certainly doesn't turn into a real dirty-nuisance sort of thing.'

'My brain is surprisingly huge,' Courier corrected her. 'And many things stick. I often know what is the main thing. I am a bit of an expert in many things. And I know at least one thing that you have forgotten.'

'What?' Florizella said snappily, for she was bored of the car and embarrassed at having three tall enchanters having a conference over her head, *and* she was hungry.

'It's lunch—'

Courier was about to say that it was lunch*time* when he was interrupted by the terrifying scream of wind through huge feathers and three Good Manner Eagles swooped down from the skies and fixed their huge claws around the children's belts, hauling them upwards. They set off with great beating wings towards the palace.

'No!' Florizella yelled. 'Not again!'

'Can't be late for lunch,' one Good Manner Eagle said.

'Got to wash your hands,' said the other.

'I'm not even invited to lunch!' Bennett shouted. 'Surely it would be rude to just turn up?'

'Oh, so it would!' said the Good Manner Eagle that was holding him, and it opened its claws and dropped him from a great height into the muck heap at the stables.

'Honestly!' Bennett said crossly as he

picked himself up out of the stinking straw and tried to brush horse poo off his clothes. 'This is ridiculous. I know good manners are important but—'

'We *are* the Good Manner Eagles,' the three of them chorused, soaring up together, dragging Courier and Florizella up and up and up.

'Come for lunch, Bennett!' Florizella yelled down. 'I'm inviting you.'

'I don't have any clean clothes to change into!' Bennett shouted back. 'And now I have straw and horse pee all over me!'

'Oh, come anyway!' echoed down from the sky.

The eagle who had dropped Bennett flew down and stood beside him. 'You can't go to lunch with the king and the queen looking like that,' it said severely. 'You're filthy.'

'Whose fault is that?' Bennett demanded crossly as the eagles holding Courier and Florizella circled higher and higher in the sky so that she and Courier were just little dangling dots under the mighty eagle wings.

CHAPTER THREE

*Courier creates a
truly brilliant invention*

s soon as the two Good Manner Eagles reached the palace front door, they dropped down out of the sky and went *SPLASH* into the moat and held Courier and Florizella under the water for what felt like a very long time. Finally, they lifted them up again, spluttering and coughing. 'What did you do that for?' Florizella demanded. 'You nearly drowned me.'

'It's good manners to wash your hands before meals,' one of the eagles told her, placing her in the courtyard before the palace front door.

'Wash your hands, yes! Not be held underwater!'

The eagle ignored her complaints. 'Now, do I have to remind you about sitting up straight and using your knife and fork?'

'You don't have to remind me of anything,' Florizella said crossly. 'In fact, I wish you wouldn't do anything at all. It's not helpful.'

The eagle looked down its big yellow beak at her. 'Is that a polite tone of voice?' he asked. 'Is that a polite tone of voice for a princess? What does Princess Rule number eight say?'

Rule no 8: Beautiful manners are a princess's greatest gift.

Florizella shut her mouth very tightly on a very rude reply.

'Do princes have to be so very polite?' Courier asked his eagle, who was holding him flat on his face under a restraining claw. 'Young princes, for example? Are beautiful manners my greatest gift?'

'No.' The eagle lifted him up and tweaked his wet clothes into place with its big beak so that it pulled him one way and another like a puppet. 'Princes have the Permit. They can pretty well do whatever they like. They ought to be noble, but day-to-day good manners – not so much.'

'Oh, so how should I be noble?' Courier asked, interested at once.

'Riding around and rescuing,' the eagle said. 'Challenging duels. Taking on dragons. Brave stuff. Fun stuff.'

'The Prince Permit! Isn't it great?' Courier said, grinning at Florizella and knowing how much it would irritate her. As her little brother, he believed (wrongly) that it was his job to be irritating now and then.

'Ridiculous, old-fashioned nonsense,' she said, and marched into the palace for lunch with her father the king and her mother the queen.

But someone else had come to lunch with the

queen. More to the point, it had come to lunch
ON the queen. When Florizella entered the
magnificent marble banqueting hall, she found
a great stake driven into the marble floor, the
king and queen tied to the stake and the Sea
Serpent from the bay of the Unscalable Cliffs
smiling at them both in a most agreeable way.

'Another princess for lunch!' it hissed when
it saw Florizella. 'And so politely punctual!' At
once, one of its powerful little forelegs shot out,
grabbed her and tied her back to back with the
king and queen on the same stake.

'And another!'

It was just about to grab Courier, when
Courier lifted one hand in a stop sign, and then
the other, like someone doing a disco-dance and
said. 'Stop right there. Thank you very much.'

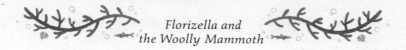
The Sea Serpent was so surprised that Courier had neither screamed nor fainted that it did stop, right where it was, and widened its beautiful blue eyes.

'I have a permit,' Courier said very firmly. 'The Prince Permit. You can't lay a hand on me; I'm a prince. You can fight me to the death, of course, but I'm assuming nobody wants to risk that. Not with me being the only son and heir.'

'Worth a go,' said the king from under the coils. 'Boys will be boys. Can't stop them! When I was a lad—'

'Of course not, Courier!' said the queen, a little breathless because the Serpent was squeezing. 'You're too precious to risk in a fight . . .'

'OK! You have the Prince Permit, so nobody

is allowed to touch you. I'll eat this one first instead,' the Serpent said, eyeing Florizella.

'Not so,' Courier said, still very confident. 'She has a permit too.'

'She can't have!' the Sea Serpent said angrily. 'She's a princess; she has to follow the Rules. She has a life cycle: Grow Up, Tied Up, Eaten Up. She's a commodity. She's a comestible. She's *my* comestible.'

'She is a new sort of princess, just as I am a new sort of prince,' Courier said quickly, inventing brilliantly as he went along. 'She doesn't obey the Rules, and I don't use the Permit. We have neither special privileges nor special duties. We're not going to be princes and princesses like people used to be in fairy tales. We're going to be fair. We're going to be equal. So she doesn't always get eaten, and I don't always fight. We can choose what we do. She doesn't have to marry and leave home. I don't get to be king of her home just because I'm a boy. It's all change.'

'This is political correctness gone mad,' said the Sea Serpent. It was truly disgusted.

The king completely agreed with it, but thought he had better not say so.

'I'm keeping my permit,' he said quietly to Courier when he thought the Sea Serpent wasn't looking. 'Best schools, best clubs, first dibs on the throne, no housework and no ME time.'

'Oh! What's ME time?' Courier asked. If he had one fault as a young prince, it was that he was very easily distracted.

'It's what they all want,' the king whispered, 'princesses and queens, women and girls; they ask for it all the time. It's time for themselves. To have a bubble bath or eat chocolates or read a book or something. I don't know what they do. I don't want anything like that. All my time is ME time. Who else's could it be?'

'Oh, I see,' Courier said. He turned to the Sea Serpent. 'Free choice on being eaten, and we all get our own ME time twenty-four hours a day.'

'What about me?' said the Sea Serpent.

'You can have ME time . . .' Courier began to offer.

'I live in the sea; I have no interest in wallowing in a bath in ME time. I meant what about my lunch?'

'You're going to have to eat anyone you find,' Courier ruled. 'You can't keep picking on princesses.'

'I'll fight you for the queen then,' the Sea Serpent offered.

Florizella struggled to get her hand on the knife in her boot under the hard grip of the Sea Serpent, but she couldn't even get near. It was going to be all down to her baby brother, and he hadn't got beyond Class 2 on swordplay yet.

'Fight me for her, would you?' Courier dared the Sea Serpent, speaking through his teeth like a hero, rather hoping the answer would be: 'Meh. Maybe not then.'

But the Sea Serpent just flared its gills and smiled.

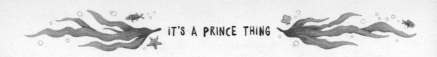

Courier looked around for help. 'Bennett?' he shouted hopefully. 'Guards? Anybody?'

CHAPTER FOUR

*In which Bennett and a Good
Manner Eagle have a major
disagreement on etiquette*

*L*uckily for Courier, Prince Bennett was
listening to all of this, heroically poised
outside, waiting for exactly the right moment
to come to the rescue. Better than that, he was
going to swing in, crash through the windows
and drop into a fighting crouch with his sword
in his hand. He took a firm grip of a long rope
looped over the highest tree, rose up to the
tip of his toes and leaped into the air for his

Big Entrance when a large hard claw grabbed him from behind, and a great beak whispered in his ear, 'Appropriate attire.'

The Good Manner Eagle had got a hold of Bennett and wasn't letting him swing anywhere.

Bennett struggled in its unbreakable grip. 'Not now! Not now!' he whispered fiercely. 'I'm rescuing the queen! I'm saving Florizella.'

The Good Manner Eagle hesitated. 'Those trousers won't do,' it said. 'I'm sure about that.

'It doesn't matter!' Bennett promised, watching the Sea Serpent in the banqueting hall flick its long tongue and slither towards Prince Courier. 'Anything! Let me go! I've got to rescue Courier! If I was stark naked, it would be OK!'

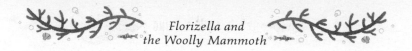

'Not stark naked surely?' the Good Manner Eagle was worried. 'I'm sure that's not acceptable.'

'I swear it, I promise it!' Bennett was dancing on the spot with impatience, held close by the eagle's great foot, which was looped through his belt. 'Look at David fighting Goliath! Stark naked except for a leaf.'

'Bennett! Anyone! Help!' Courier yelled from inside the banqueting hall as the Sea Serpent reared up before him like a giant cobra about to strike, and with a tremendous crash Prince Bennett came smashing through the tall glass window just as the Good Manner Eagle ripped every piece of dirty clothing off him. He was completely naked.

'Gosh, Bennett!' Courier said, shocked out of his fear. 'No pants?'

The Sea Serpent recoiled. 'No pink gown?'

'I say, Bennett!' the king remarked. 'Forgotten something? Too quick out of the shower this morning? Even a towel, dear boy . . .'

Bennett blushed from his face to his bottom, as they could all clearly see. He swung out again on the backswing of the rope and they heard him yelp as he jumped down into the rose bushes.

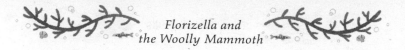

'That was a brilliant rescue plan of Bennett's,' Florizella said loyally. 'It was just a pity about his clothes.'

'It was the Good Manner Eagle!' Bennett yelled from outside. 'He tore my pants off! And now he won't give them back.'

'Oh yes – you have to have good manners,' Courier said to the Sea Serpent who – rather dazed by the sudden appearance and disappearance of a stark naked prince – had lowered its gills. 'If you have good manners, you can eat the queen one piece at a time. Start with her hand.'

He nodded to the queen who very quickly and cleverly took off her long white glove and threw it to the Sea Serpent. As it flew through the air it looked just like a hand and an arm, and she hid her real arm in the long sleeve of her dress.

'Tasty?' Courier asked the Sea Serpent.

'Mmmm! Not as chewy as I would have thought . . . no gristle,' the Sea Serpent mumbled, its mouth filled with leather glove.

'OH NO!' Courier shouted out through the smashed window. 'Here's someone talking with his mouth full! Not using his knife and fork! And not the least idea of a napkin!'

At once, the three enormous Good Manner Eagles came screaming through the broken window. One seized the Sea Serpent by its neck, another uncoiled its tail, and the third grabbed its middle, which was wrapped round Florizella and the king and queen. Together, they swooshed up into the air, without pausing

for anything, shocked to their tail feathers
by the dreadful manners of the Sea Serpent.
Without a word they flew through the
broken window and carried it far, far out
to sea.

'What about my dinner?' the Sea Serpent
shouted as they lowered it gently into the deep
ocean.

'When you have learned to behave,' one of
the Good Manner Eagles said sternly, soaring
over the waves. 'And it's called lunch.'

'Very nice meeting you,' said the other
tremendously politely.

'I hope we meet again under happier
circumstances,' said the third.

'Well, I don't,' said the Sea Serpent, and
it stuck out its long green tongue at the

Good Manner Eagles and dived deep beneath the sea before they could complain.

Bennett climbed in through the broken window. He was dressed in his ragged clothes and smelled strongly of horses. 'Sorry,' he said to Florizella. 'Sorry for being late. Sorry about before. You OK? Courier rescued you OK?'

Florizella beamed at him and hugged her little brother. 'He was great,' she said. 'And he's got a really brilliant invention.'

'Not an aeroplane?' Bennett begged. 'Tell me it's not a helicopter?'

'Better than anything like that,' Florizella said. 'He's invented that princesses and princes shall be judged for themselves, and not have to obey The Rules, and not get any Permits. But just be normal people.'

'We have to give up The Permit?' Bennett asked him. 'Courier, hold on, this might be another bad invention.'

'No, we really do,' Courier agreed. 'Or at any rate we share it. First in the lifeboats depends on who needs it most, and first into battle depends on who's the best at fighting.'

'ME time?' Florizella asked.

'Everyone's time is their own,' Courier ruled. 'Nobody has to ask for time for themselves. And anyone can be called whatever name they like, and be whoever they want to be. Everyone can wear anything they like.' He glanced at Bennett. 'Or nothing at all, if that's what they prefer.'

'That was the Good Manner Eagle!' Bennett exclaimed.

Courier shrugged. 'Express yourself!' he urged. 'I can wear a dress; you can go naked! Why ever not? Being free to be yourself is the main thing.'

Florizella nodded at Bennett. 'I told you,' she said.

'Really, this is the most unsatisfactory lunch I have ever attended,' the king complained. *'Undootedly! Undootedly!* We haven't had anything to eat, the banqueting hall window has been broken, and one of the guests arrived on a rope, stark naked. And the Good Manner Eagles have kidnapped the Sea Serpent! What is the world coming to is what I'd like to know! It looks completely frozen.'

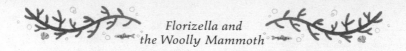

'Frozen?' Florizella asked. 'Did you say frozen? I'm sorry about there being nothing to eat, Dad, but . . .' She followed his gaze out of the window. 'Oh no,' she said.

CHAPTER FIVE

I am very glad to say there is a Mammoth in this chapter. Actually, I wish that there could be a Mammoth in every chapter

Outside the window was a complete white-out from a blizzard of snow. Through the whirling snowflakes Florizella could just make out a huge polar bear strolling through her father's rose garden, followed by people wrapped from head to toe in furs, running behind a twelve-dog sledge. The sound of excited howling and barking filled the room and Samson the wolf, who had decided long ago that he preferred being a pet dog, took one look out of the window and went quietly to sit behind the throne.

'What's happened?' Bennett came to her side. 'Wow! The weather has changed fast. It was midsummer a moment ago.'

'It must be the enchanters,' she said gloomily. 'Weren't they going to get some ice? I think they've rather overdone it.'

Courier joined them. 'This may be partly my fault,' he said. 'I don't mind owning up.'

'It's all your fault,' Florizella said crossly. 'First the stupid car, which we should never have let you invent, then the enchanters wanted to improve it instead of simply uninventing it, and now they've frozen the whole of the Seven Kingdoms to get enough ice so that you can drive around in the only car in the kingdom.'

'You won't be able to drive on ice anyway,' Bennett pointed out.

'Well, I AM the prince,' Courier said. 'Naturally, people have to put themselves out a bit. What's a little inconvenience to them, after all? Who is going to be king? Getting your own way without even asking is the whole point of the Prince Permit . . .'

And then he realised what he'd said.

'Oh.'

'Yes,' said Florizella crossly. 'Exactly. You've just invented a new sort of prince and princess, without Rules, without Permits. So it's different now. Nobody is going to put up with inconvenient royals any more. Or spoiled princes, or irritating boys.'

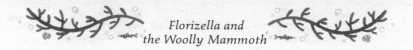

'I say!' Bennett protested very quietly.

'And one of us had better go and melt that ice. Because I'm pretty sure that there is not now, and never was, a Prince Permit that says it is OK for you to freeze the entire kingdom.'

'It's looking very bad all frozen over,' Bennett agreed. 'But in the meantime, do you think we could go sledging? Because that looks really good fun. And are those real wolves pulling the sledge? I mean, that's great, isn't it? Do you think we could tie Samson to a sledge?'

Samson came out from behind the throne and sat very tall in an obedient dog position very close to the king, as if to point out that he was nothing at all to do with wolves now. He looked sulkily at Bennett with his amber eyes.

'And now you've upset Samson!' Florizella

went to the broken window and looked out. 'I say, Bennett,' she said in a quite different voice. 'Courier, come quick! Both of you, come and have a look at this.'

The two princes crossed the room, and the king and the queen came too. They all stood in the icy blast from the broken window and looked out through the slowly clearing blizzard. Then they all jumped back, with one great leap backwards, as the most enormous, gigantic hairy Mammoth put its huge head and snowy white tusks through the window. It was so big that it blocked the light. It was quite terrifying.

'Hewwo,' he said.

CHAPTER SIX

*In which Courier learns that it
is not easy to explain extinction
to a Mammoth*

'Hello,' Courier said when no one else spoke.

The Mammoth nodded its huge head. 'Snowy,' he said, as if to make polite conversation. 'Vewy.'

'Yes,' Florizella agreed, coming forward. 'I think there's been a bit of a problem with magic. We had some enchanters who were making snow . . .'

'No, no, it's awways snowy,' the Mammoth

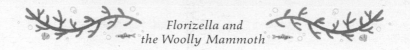

told her. 'Because it's an Ice Age.'

'It's not usually an Ice Age here,' Florizella told him. 'This is the Seven Kingdoms and it's always summer.'

The Mammoth stepped back from the gaping window, and a small blizzard of snow whirled into the banqueting room. 'You take a wook,' he recommended.

Florizella looked. For as far as the eye could see there was an unbroken plain of snow and ice. In the distance the usually green hills were mountains of snow, streaked with glaciers of ice.

'I see what you mean,' Florizella managed to say. 'This is very unusual for us.'

The Mammoth nodded. 'Not for me,' he said. 'Same owd, same owd for me. Awways snow and never Chwistmas.'

'But if the snow were to melt and the world was to get warmer, you would become extinct,' Courier pointed out. 'You would lose your hair and you would get smaller and you would be like an elephant.'

'I would not!' the Mammoth said indignantly. 'Would you shwink and wose your hair if it was sunny?'

'No, of course not! Because I'm evolved. But your children and your grandchildren and your great-great-great-grandchildren would change very slowly into elephants.'

'I haven't got childwen,' the Mammoth pointed out. 'I'm only wittle.'

'What?'

'He said he's only little.' Bennett turned to

the Mammoth. 'It's nothing for you to worry about right now.'

The Mammoth pushed its huge bulging forehead further in the window to point to Bennett with its fluffy ginger trunk. 'I wike you,' it said.

'Er, I like you too,' Bennett replied. 'Where have you come from today?'

'Have you come far?' the king asked, recognising a royal question when he heard it, and helping out in polite conversation.

'I've come from Awaska,' the Mammoth replied.

'Very nice,' the queen said, joining in. 'And what is the weather like at your home?'

'Just wike here,' the Mammoth said. 'Snow and ice, snow and ice, same owd, same owd, forever.'

'Actually, we're usually quite warm,' Florizella told the Mammoth.

'Twopical?'

'No, not hot. But warm.'

'I should wike that. I'm fweezing. I'm always fweezing. I'm compwetewy fed up of fweezing.'

Courier gave a little gasp of a giggle and then stopped himself when Florizella and Bennett both looked at him.

'You must have a hot drink,' the king said kindly. 'Let me think how we can get you inside. I don't think the front door into the palace is big enough.'

'What about the courtyard, if we put a great blanket over the top? And straw on the floor?' said Florizella.

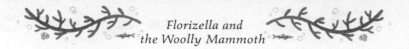

'Certainly,' said the queen, and the king hurried out to tell the pages to get the courtyard ready for a most unusual guest.

The queen turned to Florizella and Bennett. 'I'm very pleased to have one of your friends to stay, of course. It's just rather a lot of straw to have to find. And with the window broken it is terribly cold. How long do Ice Ages normally last?'

'Centuries,' Courier said helpfully. 'That's why they're called "ages". It's short for "ages and ages and ages". And when they end there is a tremendous flood.'

Bennett and Florizella exchanged a thoughtful look. 'You know,' Florizella said quietly to her friend, 'I'd rather forgotten about the flood.'

Courier helped the Mammoth over the creaking drawbridge and under the portcullis, and the king and queen had their picnic thrones set up in the courtyard among the straw, under the temporary blanket roof. Florizella and Bennett got dressed in all the winter clothing they could find and went out into the newly frozen kingdom.

The first people they saw were the three enchanters, standing under a magical sun lamp, looking out at the snowy scene.

'Frightfully sorry about this,' said the enchanter of the Seven Kingdoms.

'Our apologies,' said the orange enchanter. 'We meant to get an iceberg, but with three of

us doing the magic at once we got an Ice Age
instead.'

'And a Mammoth,' Florizella complained.
'It's very inconvenient.'

'We can reverse it at once,' the enchanter
of the Land of Deep Lakes promised her. He
raised his wand—

'Stop!' Florizella and Bennett yelled at
once. 'We've got to do something about the
Mammoth.'

'He can simply disappear,' one of the
enchanters assured her.

'I don't want him to simply disappear!'
Florizella protested.

'It is traditional,' the enchanter of the Land
of Deep Lakes pointed out. 'Isn't that the case?
That they simply disappear?'

'It wouldn't be fair,' Bennett said. 'He's only just got here. We'll have to find out if he wants to stay. He doesn't like the cold.'

'He's bored of it. Same owd, same owd,' Florizella said.

'And another thing,' Bennett said. 'How are you going to reverse the Ice Age spell?'

'We'll just melt all the ice,' the enchanter promised him.

'Have you thought about a flood?'

There was a sudden embarrassed silence. Clearly no one *had* thought about a flood.

'You'd better build an ark,' Florizella told them severely. 'Lots of arks. Enough for everyone. And one big enough for the Mammoth, before you reverse the spell.'

'How long is all this going to take?' Bennett

asked them. 'Because everyone is getting terribly cold.'

'Moments only,' the enchanter assured him. 'We'll do the arks and then we'll stop the Ice Age.'

'OK, do the arks please,' Florizella told him. 'Make sure you do enough for everyone.'

There was a swirl of icy air and, *POP*, on the top of the little hill just outside the palace gates there was a handsome ark, just like a toy ark, brightly coloured with a roof over the top deck and a gangplank so that all the animals could enter two by two. But it was huge: big enough to take a Mammoth.

And with a *POP* and then a *POP* and then a *POP* there were arks on all the hills in sight. Already people were trudging through the snow towards them, with cows and hens and cats following, and the wild animals coming along behind. Then came the extraordinary magical animals of the Seven Kingdoms that were only rarely sighted, with their frills and furs and feathers, horns and antlers and wings, and behind them came all the invisible beings that nobody ever saw at all.

Florizella and Bennett, satisfied that everyone was getting ready for the flood, went round to the courtyard to see how everyone was getting along with the Mammoth.

CHAPTER SEVEN

*In which the Mammoth
proves his point*

The king and queen and Courier were sitting on their picnic thrones in the courtyard on a huge bed of straw, having a cup of tea, and the Mammoth was sitting beside them with his trunk in a huge bucket of hot chocolate. When he saw Bennett he looked up and waggled his ears in greeting.

'Hello, everyone,' Bennett said. 'So, we've found out what has happened. The Ice Age was a mistake by the enchanters. They're very sorry, and are going to reverse it, but of course it will melt and there will be a flood, so we're all going to have to get into an enormous ark.'

'Now look here,' the king complained. 'First it was a Sea Serpent, and then it was you, Bennett, swinging in naked, and then a Mammoth and then an Ice Age, and now a flood. What I want to know, and I think I have a right to know is: am I ever going to get any lunch today?'

'In the ark,' Florizella said. 'Lunch will be served in the ark.' This was an interesting sort of lie because she did not actually know if it was true or not. It was more a statement of hope.

'Really?' the king said, brightening up. *'Undootedly?'*

'Undoubtedly,' Florizella said, moving to a

completely solid lie in order to get her parents to head towards the ark and the whole of the palace – friends, servants, animals and even little animals that nobody usually saw from mice to pixies – to follow them.

Then she turned to the Mammoth who was making an extraordinary loud gurgling, whooshing noise as he sucked the last of the hot chocolate up his trunk. It was the sort of noise you make as you finish a drink through a straw, only about a thousand times louder.

Bennett glanced nervously up at the sky, looking for the Good Manner Eagles. He thought they would have an opinion about a Mammoth hoovering up the last drops of his hot chocolate.

'I'm sorry to say this Ice Age is going to end

very quickly,' Florizella said to the Mammoth. 'I hope you don't mind?'

'I'd be gwad of it,' the Mammoth said. 'I don't wike snow or ice.'

'But will you be all right in warm weather?' Bennett asked him.

'Are you sure you wouldn't evolve?' Courier asked. 'You don't want to become an elephant by accident.'

'Aww you ever think about is ewephants,' the Mammoth complained to Courier. 'Nobody could become an ewephant by accident. It's the sort of thing you'd have to do on purpose.'

'But about the weather,' Bennett repeated patiently.

'I'd wike to be a bit hot!' the Mammoth assured them. 'Weawwy!'

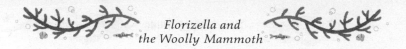
'Well, you can choose,' Bennett explained. 'You can, by magic, go back to where you came from – Alaska in the Ice Age – or you can come with us into the ark for the big defreeze and there will be a flood and when it's all over you can live here.'

'Or in Prince Bennett's kingdom, the Land of Deep Lakes,' Florizella offered quickly. 'You might like it better there.'

Bennett gave her a hard look. 'Only if he wants,' he said.

'If he evolves, he'll be much smaller,' Courier reminded them. 'It won't be like having to house and feed a Mammoth at all. It'll just be like keeping an elephant.'

'What is it with you and ewephants?' the Mammoth demanded crossly. 'Maybe you will evolve into something?'

'Actually, he has evolved a bit,' Bennett pointed out. 'He was a prince with a Permit and now he's something new, something better. He's given up the Permit so he's a fair prince. A new sort of prince. A better prince.'

'But not an ewephant!' the Mammoth said triumphantly, thinking that he had won the argument.

'At any rate,' Florizella said, 'you can stay with us in the eternal midsummer of fairytale land.'

The Mammoth raised his furry copper trunk above his head and trumpeted a happy tootle that blew a mist of hot chocolate over everyone. 'Midsummer!' he shouted. 'Faiwytale wand! Huwwah!'

CHAPTER EiGHT

Arks ahoy!

The three children and the enormous Mammoth were the last to board the palace ark. There was room enough for everyone, but the Mammoth had to stand on the bottom of the ark in the hold, with his head poking out through the hatch on the deck. The king and queen had their thrones on the quarterdeck, and Florizella, Bennett and Courier leaned over the rails and called to the enchanters. 'Is everyone aboard all the arks and nobody left behind?'

'Aye aye!' shouted the orange enchanter, who had got so excited about the arks that now he thought he was a sailor.

'Are you *absolutely* sure?' Florizella checked.

'Aye aye, captain!'

'Then reverse the Ice Age spell!' Courier cried.

The enchanters came on board and the gangplank was taken in, and everyone waited. At first there was silence and nothing happened. Then the ark, which was sitting on a mountain of ice, started to sink and sink as the ice beneath it melted. All the snow and ice around them melted too, and the land became huge lakes and great stretches of water that all joined up so that all the arks bobbed on wintry seas. It became warmer as the sun came out, and bluer as the snow clouds blew away, until it was a beautifully warm sunny day and all the arks floated around on a perfectly calm sea with no land to be seen in any direction as far as the blue horizon.

'Pleasant,' the king said. 'Very pleasant. I love a boat trip. And now, let's have lunch.'

'Right away, Your Majesty,' said the royal chef and he was moving towards the galley when he stopped in his tracks, looked out to sea and pointed a trembling finger.

'And what is the meaning of this?' came an extraordinarily cross voice, which Florizella recognised at once. 'Have you seen the size of this ocean? Where is my home? What have you done with my Unscalable Cliffs?'

'Hallo, Sea Serpent,' Courier said as the Sea Serpent reared out of the sea, flared its beautiful gills and glared at them with its wonderful sapphire stare.

'Fwightening!' said the Mammoth and ducked back under the hatch.

Courier went to the rail to talk to the Sea Serpent. 'Sorry about earlier,' he said. 'Did the Good Manner Eagles take you safely home OK?'

'No sooner did I land in the water than the whole ocean froze!' the Sea Serpent said angrily. 'I was like a fancy ice sculpture. I take it this was your doing, you miserable royal?'

'Sort of,' Courier said. 'But I didn't mean to inconvenience you. What happened when you melted?'

'I found myself in an unending waste of water, an eternity of waves, washing this way and that, like some pitiful unattached weed. I am NOT happy.'

'Me too,' said the king, hearing the last bit. '*Undootedly*! I agree with you, Sea Serpent. You'll be wanting your lunch.'

'Oh, good idea!' the Sea Serpent said. It flicked its tongue and widened its beautiful blue eyes at the queen.

She looked right back. 'Not me,' she said shortly.

'No, no,' the king said. 'You like a picnic, don't you?'

'I do,' said the Sea Serpent, flattening down its gills and speaking more sweetly, so that the Mammoth popped an eye out of the hatch to have a look.

'Ugh! What's that?' the Sea Serpent exclaimed.

'It's a Mammoth,' Florizella said. 'From the Ice Age.'

'Ridiculous,' the Sea Serpent said. 'Don't give it any picnic.'

'No, we won't,' Bennett said quickly. 'Sea Serpent, can you swim all the time, or do you need to rest on land?'

'Why?' the Sea Serpent asked, keeping a close eye on the chef, who was slicing bread for sandwiches. 'Thicker,' it said. 'I like a nice fat one.'

The queen gave him another hard, unfriendly look.

'You see, I don't think there is any land for

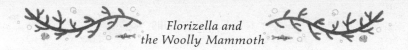

the moment,' Florizella apologised. 'This is a flood.'

'You don't say,' the Sea Serpent said, watching Courier heap a plate of sandwiches with some pies and chicken and salad. 'Not broccoli,' it said quickly.

'It's good for you,' Courier said, paying no attention and putting the plate on the highest deck so the Sea Serpent could lean over the rail and eat from the plate.

'Napkin,' the Sea Serpent said with a hard blue stare.

'Of course,' Bennett said. 'But the Good Manner Eagles are just sitting on the mast; they're not watching you. I don't think we have to be absolutely perfectly mannered in an emergency.'

'I'm not taking any chances,' the Sea Serpent said, bending its long neck so that Courier could tie a snowy tablecloth under its chin and it could start eating.

'This is better,' the king said, as the royal chef served him a big plate. Samson, who was gnawing on a big bone under the royal throne, wordlessly agreed.

CHAPTER NINE

*In which everyone aboard
discovers that even an ark
cannot fully protect you from
danger in a worldwide flood*

'The reason I asked about you needing a rest on land is because there is no land at all,' Bennett said. 'Not until the waters drain away.'

'I need my cliff,' the Sea Serpent pointed out. 'Of course I need my home. My little bay, and the Queasy Quays. The Unscalable Cliffs with the princess stake on the top, where the train turns round. Where are you going to put the princesses at lunchtime . . . ? I mean, the picnics at lunchtime,' it corrected itself with one eye on Courier, who nodded in agreement.

'Everything is all underwater,' Florizella said. 'I'm sorry, Sea Serpent, but when the ice all melted it made this tremendous flood. We're just going to have to bob about until the water drains away.'

'Well, the pirates aren't going to like that,' the Sea Serpent pointed out. 'All their treasure is buried on islands marked with a cross, and now they're underwater. How are they going to get their money? What about the violent and nasty inns? What about the treasure ships sailing for port? No ports? You're going to ruin the economy.'

'And your father isn't going to want to

eat picnics forever,' Bennett said quietly to Florizella. 'We'll have to think of a way to get the water into rivers and lakes, and the sea back to its proper size. Before dinnertime, if possible.'

'Oh, I can do that,' the Sea Serpent offered helpfully. 'On condition.'

'How would you do it?' Courier asked him suspiciously. 'And what would be the condition?'

'The condition is that I get to live in the palace moat and not be a Sea Serpent all the time,' the Sea Serpent said. 'I won't eat any of you, and the kitchen can serve my meals on the drawbridge.'

Florizella looked towards her father and mother.

'Agreed,' the queen said. 'If you really can

make the waters go down.'

'My dear,' the king said unhappily, 'are you sure about this? People already say that our kingdom is a rather peculiar place. There's Samson the palace guard dog . . .'

Samson, who was a wolf dyed blond, left his bone for a moment and came to the king and offered his paw. The king shook it absentmindedly. 'They say he's a wolf,' he said in a whisper.

'Surely not!' the queen whispered back.

'And there's Florizella who won't obey the Princess Rules,' he went on. 'And now Courier has changed the Prince Permit. And Bennett swings into lunch completely naked . . .'

'That was the fault of the Good Manner Eagle!' Bennett exclaimed.

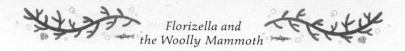

'Well, even so,' the king huffed. 'It all makes a very bad impression. Are we now going to have a Sea Serpent in the moat?'

'I think we have to,' the queen said, 'if it can get rid of the water.' She turned to the Sea Serpent. 'How *will* you do it?'

'I'll just pull out the plug,' the Sea Serpent said simply, and smiled at their amazed faces.

'The plug?' Florizella asked. 'What plug?'

'The plug at the bottom of the ocean.'

'Is there one?' Courier demanded. 'Because I don't think that's quite how oceans work.'

'Pwobably, he thinks there's an ewephant,' came a little voice from below deck.

'There is a plug, or at any rate there will be if you get the enchanters to magic one,' the Sea Serpent pointed out. 'You know, for the first

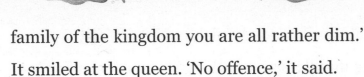

family of the kingdom you are all rather dim.'
It smiled at the queen. 'No offence,' it said.

'None taken,' she said icily.

'I see what you mean,' Bennett said. 'So we get the enchanters to magic a plug in the ocean floor, and you go down and pull it out?'

'Exactly.' The Sea Serpent gleamed at him.

'And when the sea has gone down to its usual depth you put the plug back in again?'

'High-water mark,' the Sea Serpent said cleverly.

'Right,' Courier said. 'So we'll give you a shout when the sea is at the right level, you put the plug in and you can live in the moat for as long as you like – but eating nobody.'

'Agreed!' the Sea Serpent said.

'Not a single person nor a single animal,'

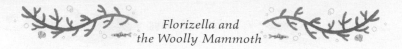

Florizella added quickly. 'Not a small one, not a middle-size one like Samson or Jellybean. You can't eat even big ones like the Mammoth.'

'Cowwect,' came a little voice from the hold of the ship.

'Agreed,' the Sea Serpent said.

'Then let's do it!' Courier said excitedly. 'Enchanters! One plug in the bottom of the ocean. Do it now, please!'

There was a flash of lightning and a sudden *GLUG*, and the Sea Serpent flared its beautiful greeny-blue gills and dived under the ship.

'Brilliant,' said Bennett.

'Just one thing,' Florizella said. 'I've just thought of something . . .'

'What?' Courier asked as he leaned over the rail, looking for the first sign of mountain or trees. 'There!' he said. 'That's the top of the Blue Mountains. Look, Father. Can you see? The top of the mountains.'

'The thing is . . .' Florizella went on.

'What?' Bennett asked. 'What are you thinking?'

'Wwwwwwhhhhhhhhhiiiiiiirrrrrllllllpooooooollllllll!'

Florizella yelled just as the ark started to sail round and round in a large circle, which became smaller and smaller as it chased itself round and round until finally it entered a spiral and went down the side of the whirlpool towards the open plug, which led to . . . who knew!

CHAPTER TEN

*In which everyone is
glad that Sea Serpents
can hear underwater*

'W w w w w w h h h h h h h h i i i i i i –
r r r r l l l l l p o o o o o o l l l l l l !'
screamed Florizella, Bennett, Courier, the
king, the queen and every person, animal and
being on board as their ship was sucked at
tremendous speed down the spiral wall of the
whirlpool – just like the one you have in your
bath, only infinitely, indescribably bigger and
faster. It was so big that the ark went round

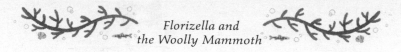

and round and started to point nose down, so fast that everyone had to cling to each other and to the rails of the ship not to fall off, so huge that all the arks, one after another, got sucked in and spun faster and faster towards the enormous mysterious hole at the bottom where the Sea Serpent waited with the plug in its smiling mouth to be told when to put it in, because enough water had drained away.

That was when Courier wished they had invented and tested a code word for putting the plug in the hole. They were all screaming 'whirlpool' and no one was shouting to the Sea Serpent to plug the drain. Courier tried to catch his breath, he tried to signal by waving, but he did not dare take both hands from the rail at once for fear of floating away. And that was when the Mammoth, most upset, most shaken and very disturbed, put his head out of the hatch and bellowed in his loudest and most indignant yell:

'Enough awweady!'

And fathoms down, on the ocean floor, the Sea Serpent heard him.

And put in the plug.

All at once, the sea was calm, and the ark bobbed to the surface, where they found themselves floating in the bay of the Unscalable Cliffs. The sun was shining, birds flew into their newly washed green trees, and all around them the other arks were settling on the tops of hills and in high green meadows. Those that were still afloat set a course to the Queasy Quays to dock beside the pirate ships. The pirates were very glad that the land had reappeared and performed a little pirate dance in their waterlogged boots.

The royal ark was still at sea when the Sea Serpent appeared on the portside bow. 'All well?' it asked, smiling.

The king, rather shaken, said, 'We were nearly sucked down the plughole!'

'You should have thought of that first,' the Sea Serpent said airily.

'*Undootedly!*' the king said with feeling. '*Undootedly* we should.'

'But you will remember our agreement,' the Sea Serpent reminded him. 'I'm glad to have my bay back, and I see that my home is undamaged, washed out rather nicely actually, but I shall live in your moat whenever I like.'

'Oh, very well,' said the king. 'I did agree it.'

'So shall we go home, dear?' the queen asked. 'The train seems to be running.'

They looked towards the shore and there was the seaside train that ran from the palace all through the little villages and towns to the seaside. As the guard opened each door, a small wave of water splashed out, but apart from that the train was ready to depart.

'Very well,' said the king.

The ark let down the great gangplank to the beach, and all the animals and people, and even the invisible beings, disembarked and boarded the train to go home.

CHAPTER TEN AND A HALF, REALLY

A very short chapter to explain how they all lived happily ever after

'I think the Mammoth is too big for the train,' Florizella said to Bennett.

'And anyway, where's he going?' he asked.

'I have an idea,' Courier said.

'No!' the other two said sternly. 'Whatever idea it is, Courier, the answer is "no".'

'Let's ask the Mammoth what sort of place he would like to live in,' Florizella said. 'And then we can take him there.'

The Mammoth was standing on the beach, piling up sand for huge sandcastles with his trunk.

'Mammoth,' said Bennett, 'what sort of place would you like to live in? Would you like to be in a hayfield and eat hay? Or perhaps be near a fruit farm and eat fruit? Would you like to live near the palace? Or somewhere quieter? What sort of place would you prefer?'

'I wather wike it here,' the Mammoth said. He waved at the sandy beach, at the stalls selling fruit and ice creams, at the river of fresh water that flowed into the beach, and the fields and woods behind it, and the bridge that ran across it to the town market. 'I wike this.'

'Could he stay here?' Bennett asked Princess Florizella. 'It's your kingdom.'

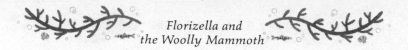

'It's our kingdom,' Florizella said nicely.

'Yes, we're going to share it,' said Courier.
'And we could have a Mammoth here, couldn't
we?'

'Yes. But where would you sleep?' Florizella
asked the Mammoth.

He pointed his huge trunk at a parasol.
'Here! Could I have an umbewewwa?'

'Yes,' Bennett replied. 'Actually, we could
make you a little tent if you would like.'

'I would wike! I would wike that!'

'And what would you eat?' Florizella asked.

'Ice cweam,' the Mammoth said as if it
were obvious. 'Mammoths wike ice cweam.'

'And what would you do all day?' Courier
asked.

'Give wides,' the Mammoth promised them.

'You know, I think this would work,' Courier said. 'And we could come to see him often, and he could help the lifeguard watch the swimmers, and he could put out the sunbeds.'

'Agweed,' said the Mammoth.

The guard of the train blew his whistle, the train gave an 'All aboard!' hoot, and Bennett said, 'Time to go!'

'I could give you a wide?' the Mammoth offered. 'Wight now! Back to the pawace?'

'Thank you!' Florizella said. 'That would be fun.' She waved the train off and it started down the track.

Courier had an idea. 'You could tow little carriages along the train track,' he suggested. 'Perhaps I could invent some sort of bicycle that you could pedal?'

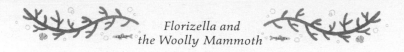
'NO!' Florizella and Bennett said at once. 'No inventions.'

The Mammoth stood beside the high lifeguard seat and first Courier and then Florizella and last of all Bennett climbed up the ladder and settled themselves behind the Mammoth's ears, in the warm safe part of his thick fluffy neck. Then the Mammoth turned towards the beautiful setting sun, and they followed

the

little train

all the

way home.

The End